Acolyte

Part Two of the Sistema Series

A DYSTOPIAN HORROR

ULTAN BANAN

ACOLYTE

Under the ocular sky of the leaden city he felt the terror and thrill of young desire. His legs trembled. The boy clung to the sill of the tiny window, his feet perched on the balcony wall. Alone, a chary bird in the night's dark, he gazed wide-eyed through the glass, straining to see through the tattered blinds. Inside, in the tub, was the girl. Only seconds before he'd watched her undress and slip into the water. His heart thumping for all he'd seen and all he saw now only in his mind's eye. He faltered, teetering in his illicit perch, but hung on with all his strength. Her hair sodden from the neck down clinging to her pale shoulders. Her knees, bruised and scratched, poking from the water. And rising just above the water line the shallow cleft that divided one small breast from another. The boy had not breathed since she'd sunk into the soapy water. His eyes darted one to the other through the small tear in the blinds, seeking the best vantage. The girl took a breath and submerged herself below the water. The boy started, eyes agape. He glanced at the door behind her. Then at the floor where her clothes lay scattered; poking out from beneath her shorts, one crumpled Converse sneaker. The red sweater, the one with the tear right below the arm that he liked to poke her through, an action that always elicited a squeal and an excitable shudder. He'd seen her in the red sweater that morning from the vantage of his bedroom as she left her apartment, and then again in the afternoon when she left school as he watched from the tree in the park. He'd wanted to go and talk to her but she was with friends, and three girls were two too many. No, he liked it best when they were alone.

The girl burst from the water, gasping for air. Her tiny pointed breasts emerged for a single, beatific moment, before dipping back below the water line. The boy shook, almost falling from his nesting place. Her hair clung to her face and she brushed it from her eyes, then she spat into the tub. The boy's fingers were numb and his legs were shaking something terrible. A leg rose up, and for a moment he got a glimpse of the girl's disfigured foot. Then, as if aware of being watched, she plunged it back into the water. He'd seen it only once, when he'd let himself in the apartment that afternoon when she was alone and the door was left open, and he'd found her on the couch with a thin blanket over her, dreaming god-only-knows-what dreams, her mouth half-open and arm flung up behind her head. The smell of her father in the room. Her two feet poked from the blanket, and he saw it then, the poor scarred foot that she worked so well to hide. She hardly even limped – you had to look closely to see it. He didn't care. If anything, it made his perturbed heart beat all the more for her. He'd watched for some minutes that time, and then he'd snuck back out and closed the door, knowing somehow he'd seen too much. He stored the vision away, and it was the object of affection in many long nights of his imagination… one night he'd lay her on the bed next to him and take her foot and anoint it with holy oil, and since he didn't know the gradations of oil's holiness, it would be the top-shelf olive oil from the Italian's store he'd do the anointing with. Another night he'd cover it with kisses and tell her it was the most beautiful part of her, even if he knew he'd never say it in real life, because that kind of thing might land him in trouble. Or he might lay close to it and whisper secrets to it, knowing

2

the girl would not hold against him the jealous confidence between him and her scarred limb, but rather appreciate and respect that he held it in such high esteem and trust, and would love him all the more for it. Yes, he had many things yet to show her. But first, she must trust him fully.

The girl's head jerked upward and to the right, as if hearing a noise. The boy's stomach tightened. Her hands, soaping her slim calf, paused, then continued but at a pace cautious, over her glistening skin. The boy could hardly hold on. He clung desperately to the windowsill. The girl froze then, and seconds later, the bathroom door opened. Unmistakably her eyes flitted to the small window then down at the floor as her father appeared in the open door. She looked up at her father then down at her knees, her hands sliding onto her bony joints, her shoulders curving in to protect her small frame. She bit her lip. The boy, his stomach in knots and his lip quivering, slipped and fell to the floor with a hissed curse. Without a pause, he leapt over the dividing wall of the balcony to the other side, gripping the downspout and shimmying in a flash up to the third floor in the dark of night. He reached his own balcony and slipped in through the open door, his head filled with desire, angst and loathing, and much besides.

From spyings such as these would come his purpose.

2

The knock woke him and he rolled over in the bed and closed his eyes. The voice of his mother came through the door.

'Caleb? Are you in there?' A pause. 'I know you're in there, I heard you come in. Caleb...'

Knowing it wouldn't stop he silently turned and slid from the bed and stood up and kicked on his sneakers. The door handle dipped but it was locked from the inside. The boy grabbed his coat and his bag and went to the balcony door.

'Caleb?'

He paused momentarily before sliding it open and slipping outside, and in seconds, he was on the downspout and sliding toward the ground below. He hit the ground with both feet and dashed away.

At the Italian deli he walked right on by. The old man would be behind the counter and he'd chased him from the store only a week ago, so he went on down to the Korean store on the corner and slipped in the door in the wake of two ghetto kids he knew would draw attention away from him. Inside, he scanned the place. Three or four customers. One guy at the register. He stole down the back aisle and rifled a few cinnamon rolls and a tin of soda, slipping them into the pockets of his oversized army jacket. Then he waited for the ghetto kids to head for the register, and when they were in front of the clerk he pocketed a candy bar and a couple of licorice chews and walked right out the door. Didn't look back. The clerk never even saw him.

He crossed the road and went into the park and sat under the tree where he'd wait for the girl. She'd be along soon enough. He took the phone from his bag and looked at the time, and put it away again. He opened a cinnamon roll and the tin of soda and ate and drank and watched the street. Across the road, the Italian's wife was hanging out the window of their third-floor apartment shaking the bedsheets. He chewed on the roll and watched her: big and old, humungous breasts contained tightly within her blue and white floral dress, her hair white and short and her face with the scowl of one who's worked a lifetime serving customers on the wrong side of town. He followed the track of the steps up the side of the building to her window as he rolled up the empty packet and tossed it at his feet. The sound of whistling caused him to turn. Seeing Vince approach, he cursed silently.

'Whaddup,' said the lanky teenager who plonked himself down on the grass next to him.

'Hey.'

'You got another one of those?' Vince pointed at the empty packet that lay unfurling in the grass at his feet.

Reluctantly, the boy slipped a hand in his pocket and took out his other roll and handed it to the kid. He stuck his hand in his other pocket and took out the candy bar and began to demolish it.

'Didn't see you last night. Where were you?' Vince said as he peeled open the cinnamon roll.

The boy shrugged. 'At home. Didn't feel like coming out.'

'Yo, you missed some shit, I'm telling you. We riled up GB and his buddies last night right over there while they were trying to work. He lost his shit and chased us clean out of the park and into the street, and get this, we flew out in front of traffic, I almost got hit by a fucking car, and Jonesy slipped down the empty manhole on the other side there and caught his leg and it snapped clean in two, right here…' Vince gestured with a chopping motion to the middle of his calf, right on the shinbone. 'Clean broke it in half. The bone was sticking out and everything, a big jagged fucking thing and blood was everywhere…'

The boy didn't say anything.

Vince looked at him. 'What do you think of that, huh?'

'Jonesy's a douche.'

'He's in fucking hospital man with his leg broke in two. Have some sympathy.' He fell quiet and proceeded to eat the cinnamon roll, then continued with his mouth full. 'I swear, Steve disappeared pretty quickly after that – I've never seen him move so fast. You know what a big fat fucker he is. And his crew cleared out pretty sharpish. Their spot was open all night. Man, if we'd had a bit of gear, we'd have *cleaned up*.'

He turned to look at the can between the boy's legs.

'Any of that left?'

The boy was one step ahead. He held it up and shook it, the dribble at the bottom rattling off the walls of the empty tin. He placed it back between his open legs. The kid tossed his wrapper over his shoulder.

'What you doing tonight?' Vince said.

The boy shook his head. 'Dunno.'

'Wanna go out and try for this place I've been scoping?'

'What is it?'

Vince shrugged. 'It's just a dingy apartment with this old guy living there. But get this…' He leaned in. '…they say he's got a whole collection of vintage porno stuff, magazines and the like, know what I mean? Could be worth something…'

The boy looked puzzled. 'Old magazines?'

'*Vintage* magazines. They say some of them are worth like a hundred bucks. And maybe cash too, I dunno. Wanna see if we can work the place?'

'Who else?' the boy said.

'Just you and me. Fuck those other guys. We only have to

split it two ways. What do you say?'

The boy plucked at the grass in front of him, all the while looking out into the street. 'Who are you gonna sell it to?'

'Never mind. Just you leave that to me. I know one or two old dudes who might buy it. You just need to help me steal it.'

The girl appeared then. Down the street he caught sight of her through the park railings, saw the yellow jumper and knew her as intimately as he knew his own mother. He knew all her clothes, what little of them she had. And even if it wasn't the bright primary colors, he'd still have known her ruffled dirty fair hair from anywhere.

'What do you say, dude?'

'What? Yeah sure. Okay.'

He watched as she crossed the street with Shelley and they came together arm in arm along the sidewalk and crossed his path, all the while she looking through the railings at him and waiting for him to register her appearance. She held up a hand and shook a few shy fingers at him. He blushed and raised a hand. He wished Vince wasn't there. But even if the boy had been alone, she wouldn't have approached him. They were shy in company both. With a final look at him she disappeared out of sight and into the school. The boy looked at the ground. Beside him, the kid grinned.

'You fingered her yet, dude?'

Blood suffused the boy's face, and when he looked up Vince recoiled at the look in his eye.

'Jesus, sorry man. Forget I asked.' Vince stood up and brushed the grass from his jeans and stuck his hands in his pockets. 'So like, tonight, yeah?'

The boy looked away and nodded. 'Sure.'

Vince moved his neck chicken-like in acquiescence. 'Let's not meet here. I don't wanna see GB. I'm not afraid of him or anything, but I don't need the hassle.'

'Where do you wanna meet?'

'The guy lives on Eastway. Know the old army store next to the shut-up Chinese place?'

'Yeah.'

'Meet me there at ten.'

'Okay.' The boy looked up briefly and then turned away.

'Okay dude. See you later.'

Vince turned, hands in pockets, and shuffled away, the chain hanging from his pockets rattling against his thigh. The boy plucked up a handful of grass and cast it into the morning air.

When he crossed the underpass later that night heading in the direction of Chinatown, there were patrol cars everywhere. He left Duke Road to take the side streets, cutting down the filthy alleyways filled with debris, excrement and the rotting detritus of the city. The boy was no stranger to these back streets and had made many an escape through the darker and more unfrequented thoroughfares of the city. Two tottering alcoholics turned as he passed them, but seeing no hesitation or fear in the boy they didn't accost him. After a bit the boy turned down an alley heading back in the direction of Duke Road. He stopped to take a piss then moved on. About halfway down the alley he heard something fall from above him, maybe plaster or gravel. He stopped to look up. Five stories above him, in the dark and silhouetted against the dull blue-grey of the sky was the figure of a boy, not much older than him. The figure stood on the edge of the building as if preparing to jump. The boy's first thought was: *A suicide*. He moved instinctively back against the wall, still peering up into the dark abyss above him. The figure, carved out of the skyline, didn't see him. His attention seemed beholden to whatever distant vista lay out in front of him. The boy clutched the strap of the bag over his shoulder and stared enraptured at the figure. Unaware of each other's presence, yet caught entwined in some unwritten, unfinished drama. Or perhaps the outcome was already written. For the boy there was some unquantifiable sense of inevitability about the scene. Almost like he'd seen it before. Like déjà vu but with no sense of disorientation. Like he was watching a reel, a mundane replay of some colorless yet precipitous life event. He almost raised a hand to swipe at the scene, so still and untouched and illusory it seemed. And then, breaking the spell, the boy perched on the edge above him bent at the knees, and in a seemingly impossible leap, thrust himself into the air in the direction of the building by whose wall the boy stood. Then he vanished. The boy stared up into the air for a long time, then looked down, and looked up again as if what he'd just seen was unreal, a mirage, some kind of night vision. He turned and walked down the alley.

When he emerged onto Duke Street he was right opposite the Chinese takeaway. Police cars were outside it and the doorway was halfway raised. An officer emerged from the door bent at the knees and speaking into a walkie-talkie clipped to his shirtfront. The boy's eyes darted up and down the street and along the alley that ran down the side of the Chinese. If Vince hadn't scarpered already he'd be hiding in the alley. The boy turned right and headed down Duke Street, and about a hundred meters down crossed the street and turned back on himself. A few disinterested onlookers were standing watching the police at a distance, and these he passed, coming to a stop behind a van that was parked just beyond the first police cruiser. He waited, watching. And when the officer with the walkie-talkie nipped back under the shutters and the single officer outside turned her back, he slipped out from behind the van and down the alley.

He found Vince at the end of the alleyway, perched on a first-floor balcony watching the activity. He was biting his nails as he turned to see the boy climb on top of a bin and leap to take hold of the steps to pull himself up. In seconds, he was crouching next to Vince on the rusted steel balcony.

'What's going on?' he whispered.

Vince shrugged. 'Dunno. Prob'ly some junkie crawled in there and OD'ed or something.'

'I guess we should hold off on the old man's place.'

'Are you kidding? This is the perfect cover. They'll never reckon a place be raided right under their noses.'

'Yeah, but what if he calls the cops? They're right there, right outside.'

Vince waved a hand. 'They'll be gone in five minutes. Don't worry.' He stood and looked skyward. 'Come on, we'll get a look at the place.'

Vince hopped onto the steps that rose up the side of the building toward the roof and began to climb. The boy followed. They ascended three floors to the roof above. Vince moved along the roofline at a crouch, while the boy stepped up onto the parapet wall and looked out over the alley, then down into the darkness below. He teetered there, assessing the distances and assessing the fall, and wondering. Vince, having turned back, arrived at his side.

'Yo, what the fuck are you doing?'

The boy stepped back from the ledge, turning and putting a hand on Vince's arm and pushing him gently.

'Come on.'

When they reached the Duke Street side of the building they looked out over the edge and down into the street. The curious that had gathered to watch the police had now moved away or were in the process of doing so. Outside the Chinese, three officers were in the street standing in a clique. The two boys turned their heads at the flashing lights. An ambulance had turned onto the street and was heading their way.

'Told you,' Vince said as the ambulance rolled silently down the quiet street and pulled up right outside the Chinese. Two medical staff got out and opened the ambulance and took out a body bag. They exchanged brief and cursory words with the officers and proceeded into the Chinese with little ceremony. Minutes later they emerged, the black body bag laden and swinging between them. They placed it on a gurney in the back of the ambulance and closed it up.

'What a way to go,' Vince said, 'junked out in some dirty,

abandoned Chinese. Guy was probably half-eaten by rats by the time they found him.'

'Maybe it was a girl,' the boy said.

'What a waste.'

The boy turned his attention from the events below and gazed down the building. 'Where's our place?'

'This one, right below us.' Vince gestured with his chin.

A thin light spilled out onto the balcony below the windows, the flickering of a TV apparent against a brass watering can that sat on a crate on the rusted balcony floor.

'Think he's awake?'

'I guess. If we're lucky, he'll be drunk and passed out. Then we can just grab what we want and get the hell out. He won't know a damned thing.'

'Sounds easy.' The boy put a finger in his ear and shook it. Below in the street, the ambulance pulled away and the last police officer emerged from the takeaway followed by an Asian man. The officer spoke to him as he lowered the shutter and padlocked it to an anchor and rattled it to check it was shut.

'See? They're all out of here,' Vince said. 'Now's our time.'

One of the patrol cars had already pulled away and was heading down Duke Street. After a few final words, the last officer got in his car and the Asian guy got in the van and drove away. The patrol car didn't move.

'Fuck these guys,' Vince said. 'Come on and we'll scope the place out.'

The boy hesitated as Vince climbed onto the steps and shimmied down to the balcony. He looked up at the boy and opened his eyes wide as if to say, *What are you waiting for?* The boy hopped onto the ladder and followed his friend to the balcony below. They stood crouched on either side of the window, the TV flickering in the room beyond the wall. Vince raised his head and peered into the room. It was empty. Of people, at least. But a hoarder lived there. Junk was piled wall to ceiling, the floor a grim carpet of refuse and dirt.

'Holy shit, look at the state of this place.'

The boy peeked inside. He shook his head. 'Are you kidding me? How are we supposed to find anything in this mess?'

Below in the street the lights of the police cruiser came on and the sirens too, and both boys froze and gazed down into the street as the car pulled away from the curb and sped down the street heading in the direction of Chinatown. The boys turned back to the window.

'Tell me something, dude. Because I'm about ready to climb down here and go home.'

Vince put a hand on his arm. 'I swear, this guy's got stuff. For the taking. It's all in his bedroom, in a cabinet, but the key's in the lock and it's ready to empty.'

'How do you know all this?'

'My old man used to know him back in the day. I heard him talking to one of his buddies about the collection. I swear, it's in there.' He turned to look inside. 'We just need to get through all this *shit*…'

The boy took a breath as he scanned the room. It looked like a lost cause. But they'd come all this way. Just maybe there'd be a few bucks in it.

'Let's go look at the kitchen.'

Vince gestured with his head to the balcony behind the boy which ran around the wall to the other side of the building. The boy turned and went squatting around the corner, the balcony beneath him giving a very faint bounce. On the other side was a door and another window. Vince, coming behind the boy, tried the door and found it locked. But the upper sash of the window was open a crack. He stood up and pulled it out. It was on a restrictor and only opened about a hand's length. Vince turned to the boy.

'You can get through there.'

'There's no fucking way.'

'Course you can. It's a squeeze, but you can do it. No way I'm getting through.'

'Through there?'

'Trust me, you can make it in. And when you're inside you just pop the door for me.'

The boy looked up at the window. A night breeze blew around them and the sound of music came from an apartment a floor or two below. A waft of cigarette smoke. The boy stood up and tried the door again, then grumbling, hoisted himself up onto the window ledge. Vince stood behind him and put a shoulder under his thigh.

'I got you,' he said.

The smell from inside hit him. Smells familiar which made him uneasy. He tried to crack the window open further but it wouldn't budge. He put his ear to the opening and listened for some sound from inside. All he heard was the TV.

The boy looked down at Vince. 'What if he comes in and finds me?'

Vince shook his head. 'As soon as you hit the floor, pick something up – a pan or anything. If someone appears, smack them with it and get the hell out.'

The boy turned back to the window and slid his two arms inside and pushed his head through. Then his shoulders. The smell stronger now. It made him angry and he didn't know why. He pushed with his feet up off the window ledge until his chest was in. Now it was a matter of getting down without making a noise. The sink below the window was stacked with dirty dishes. As he pushed through, the handle dug into his back painfully. He grimaced, forcing himself through the small gap until he was in up to the waist. He reached the sink and put his hands on the edge of the counter and pulled himself inside upside down: first his right leg, and he planted his foot against the window frame, then his left, and when both legs were in he kicked off the window frame and twisted his body, coming to land on the floor with both feet but spilling onto his ass. He froze, unmoving, his heart pounding. He looked up at the window. Vince peered down at him, eyes wide and mouth open dumbly. The boy sat listening for what seemed like a small eternity, and when he heard no movement from

14

inside the house he pushed himself to his feet. He looked at the door into the living room, then he turned to look at Vince. Vince held up his hands in a gesture of confusion and pointed at the balcony door, but the boy turned away. He crept to the living room door and peered in. Vince knocked on the window. The boy turned and told him with his eyes to stop.

In the room, the TV hummed. Some panel show, low jokes and inanities and canned laughter. Seeing the room in its entirety and seeing that no one was there, the boy took a final look over his shoulder at Vince and slipped inside.

That smell again, crawling into the boy and causing his throat to close. He raised his sleeved hand to his nose and covered it. With his free hand, he lifted a screwdriver that sat wedged in the sofa and held it in his hand like a blade. A cursory glance around the room told him there was nothing here worth stealing. And he wasn't about to start digging through the junk that was piled in every corner. Next to the TV, a vintage stroller, and inside it a large bust of Stalin. The boy looked for a desk or drawers of some sort but saw none. He turned to the far door. Stepping out into the hall, the smell intensified. He grew more uncomfortable. The hallway was in darkness and he could discern to his right from the lights beyond the window a small bathroom. To his left, the door only partially closed, the bedroom. He raised the screwdriver and opened the door with his elbow, the blood pounding in his head and the boy fighting a tumultuous trembling in his limbs.

The sight of the man in the chair stopped him cold. He stared straight at the boy, but it took the boy some seconds to realize it was with cold dead eyes the man stared. The boy was still standing with the screwdriver held in front of him. Coiled in an offensive stance, he returned the dead man's stare, as if he expected the dead guy to rise from the chair and advance on him. When it was clear there was to be no confrontation, the boy relaxed, dropped his hand, and walked toward the body.

The man was in his late fifties, dressed in pants and a formal shirt that was unbuttoned, as if he'd been getting ready for a meeting and thought better of it, sitting down half-dressed and giving up the ghost. There was a look of despair on his face, as if his final moments had been filled with some terrible revelation. The boy tried to lift the man's arm, finding it frozen with rigor mortis, but lifted it a few inches nonetheless and let it fall with a dead slap onto the wooden armrest. He looked at the man. He was ugly in a way beyond appearances. The boy's mouth folded in a grimace and he turned to the folding desk at the end of the bed. He opened it, his eyes alighting on the roll of bills there. He looked over his shoulder at the door before lifting it and cramming it inside his jacket. He rifled the desk but found only paper. Then he turned to the wardrobe that ran across the back wall, which the corpse guarded like a sedate and unmoving sentry. The boy pushed the sliding door open to reveal, on one side, the man's shabby assortment of clothes, and on the other, the collection for which they'd come. From floor to ceiling was a lurid assortment of VHS tapes, magazines, reels, photo albums and memorabilia, and much more. The boy slipped one magazine from the shelf and flicked through it before dropping it in disgust. Then he turned to the glass cabinet which was built into the wardrobe. These were the things he wanted, he was sure of it. He looked hurriedly in the desk for a key, but seeing none he raised the handle of the screwdriver and brought it with force against the glass, shattering it and showering glass over the floor. He took the light backpack from his shoulder and proceeded to cram it with the contents of the case, not stopping to look at what he pulled out. When the bag was full, he slung it on his back and turned to go. He stopped in front of the dead man. Something compelled him to look into his face again. He looked into the dead eyes and the rough unshorn face with the waxen skin and the taut, despairing look about him, and he felt a tight hatred well up in him. His eyes roved over the man's body to his swollen belly, then back up to the face. The

16

boy put a hand in the man's mouth and lifted his upper lip, seeing the gold teeth there. He took out his finger and wiped it on his coat in disgust. He looked at those eyes again, realizing who the man reminded him of, and the smell and the air of neglect and despondence. It was the girl's father. Or maybe his own father. With rage swelling from some unknown and buried place inside him, he lifted the screwdriver and stabbed the man in the face, and losing himself in the fury he did it again and again, the screwdriver catching him in the eye and the neck and everywhere in between until his face was a pockmarked plateau of bloodless holes. Panting, the boy ceased and looked at the holes that gave forth no blood as the man's body fell sideways and forward. The boy noticed something he'd not seen before – a wire, running from the back of the man's neck and into his open shirt and down into a small device that he held in his hand. The boy clawed open the frozen hand and extracted the thing; it looked like a small remote of some sort with an LCD screen. He tugged at the wire and followed it to the back of the man's neck. Seeing it was embedded in the skin, he pulled out the cable where it was plugged into the device and slipped the device into his pocket. He looked with disgust at the man again, then turned and went out the door.

A knock at the front door as he was going back into the living room caused him to freeze. He looked over his shoulder at the solid wood door behind him, but when the knock turned to a thump he sprinted through the living room to the kitchen. He thought he heard someone call as he struggled to open the balcony door. Vince was watching him through the window, his face twisted with frustration.

The boy pulled the door open and darted outside.

'Yo, what the fuck man?' Vince said. 'Why'd you leave me out here?'

'We need to get out of here.'

'What? What the fuck—?'

The sound of the door crashing in caused the two of them

to freeze. Then the boy grabbed Vince by the arm and pulled him around the corner where he threw himself onto the ladder and climbed furiously to the roof. Vince followed. When they got to the roof, the two of them sprinted to the other end of the building.

'Who the fuck is that?' Vince wheezed breathlessly.

The boy ran on. 'I dunno. I don't care. Let's just get outta here…'

They descended into the alley the way they'd come, hurried down it and pelted across Duke Street, disappearing into an alley on the other side of the road.

Above the street, unseen, two figures peered from the window of the dead man's apartment.

3

The knock at the door came soft and timid.

'Caleb?'

It was well after midnight. Long past her sleeping time. He could feel her presence on the other side of the door, even as he wished she wasn't there. Something about her simply being there filled him with guilt.

'Caleb? Please – open the door.'

He sat up in the bed and looked out the balcony window. It was dark. Off in the distance he saw the faltering neon signs of the Chinese Theater flicker like the broken lamps of a garish brothel, the indecipherable hieroglyphs announcing some arcane performance of a bygone and forgotten time. He watched the signs, for a moment recalling how those lights enchanted him as a child; the bemagicked flicker of the lamps spoke of the unquantifiable mysteries and fluid zones of an outpost on the periphery of all he knew and felt safe within, acting as both the limits of his world and a caution against what lay without. Often he'd begged his father to take him to see what nebulous monolith stood there. His father never did. Perhaps he knew the child would be disappointed by the reality. Maybe he just wanted to retain the magic. Or perhaps he didn't care. Either way, now and again the boy would look out and be stirred by some mirage the theater still represented.

The knock came again soft but she didn't say his name.

He stood up and went to the door, and stood there with his hand against it, listening, listening to his mother's silence. Then he opened the door.

She didn't smile. She didn't glower at him either. Her timidity made him angry.

'I made food for you,' she said.

'I'm not hungry.'

'I know that's not true. You're always hungry.' She attempted a smile. Then she gestured with her head to the kitchen. 'Come on. Let's get some food into you.'

He followed her out, pulling the door of his room shut behind him. In the kitchen he sat down at the table. She went to the stove and spooned a huge serving of noodles into a bowl, lathered it with hot sauce and stuck a fork in it. She put it on the table in front of him and he went at it without hesitation. She watched.

Further and further apart was the time alone she got with her son. Often she was called to the school and she'd sit in the principal's office with Caleb by her side as it was explained to her that should things continue as they were then he'd end up in jail or worse, and it was a good long time before she stopped going when she was called into school. Not because she didn't love him, but because it was exhausting, and every tirade she had to listen to only chiseled another piece from her weary soul. There's a point at which overwrought mothers must resign themselves to fate, and she'd reached that point and was all the more weary for the knowledge of it.

'How've you been?'

He looked up from his food but didn't answer.

'You know I can't be here for you all the time, don't you? It's not that I don't want to, and I know you don't want it anyway, you want to be independent, but what with two jobs and…'

She trailed off, and looked down at her hands where she was digging under the nail of one thumb with the other.

'I love you, Caleb,' she said, tentatively but with tenderness.

The boy tensed up. He kept eating.

'Do you need anything? You're not getting into trouble, are you?'

He shook his head.

'You know I don't get in until late, so I hardly see you. I worry about you.'

The boy put his fork into the noodles and looked up at her and finished chewing.

'I'm okay Mom. I promise.'

She smiled. 'I really do worry. What'd you get up to tonight?'

'I was out with Vince. We were just bullshitting around.'

She shook he head. 'Caleb, get yourself some real friends. That kid's just using you.'

'He's a good guy,' the boy said.

'He's a petty thief.'

The boy slumped in his chair, his eyes sneaking toward the door. His mom sat forward, holding out her hands. 'I'm sorry. Finish eating.'

The boy eyed her before picking up the fork.

'Have you been to school?'

He shook his head.

'I wish you'd go to school.'

The boy kept his eyes on the noodles and no more was said on the matter. His mom got up, picking up her cup and going to the kettle to top it up. She sat down again. Her fingers danced nervously over the table. The tic of an ex-smoker.

When the boy finished he put the fork in the bowl and looked toward the fridge. His mom got up and went to the fridge and poured him a glass of milk and put it on the table. She sat down and watched as he emptied the glass. He put it on the table and looked at his mother then looked at his hands.

'I'm free on Saturday,' she said hopefully. 'Wanna do something together? See a movie or something?'

'I dunno if I can,' he said. Even as he said it he felt wracked with guilt.

His mom feigned a smile. 'Okay. If you can. See how you feel.'

'Thanks Mom,' he said. He got up to go. As he neared the door she said, 'Caleb, you'd tell me if something was wrong, wouldn't you?'

He turned. 'Yeah.' Then he went out.

The lock in his bedroom door shut with a kind of abortive intent.

'I can't believe you locked me out of my own fucking job, man,' Vince said as they made their way along Eastway, only minutes from where they'd ransacked the apartment the night before.

'I was only making sure there was no one home,' the boy said. 'Then I came across the stash and thought I'd save you the trouble.'

'You sure you didn't find anything else?'

'I told you—'

Before he could finish Vince grabbed a fistful of the boy's coat and stopped him dead. 'I swear, if I find out you've been holding out on me—'

The boy pushed him off. 'Get the fuck off me. I told you, I didn't find nothin'…'

Vince eyed him squarely before turning and cutting down a side street that took them toward the Sprawl.

The Sprawl was a corner of the city comprised of two streets and the alley between them. A slice of times former, it was now nothing but a skid row of sex shops, shebeens, tattoo parlors and all manner of illicit AI dens, and the worst of the city's petty criminals. The boy followed Vince into the alley. An assortment of down and outs watched their going. One guy kicked off the wall as they passed under a rusted signage which spanned the two sides of the alley.

'Hey what you lookin' for, kid? I got it, got whatever you

want. Come here to me, I got some business for ya...'

Vince threw him a wary look and walked on. The stranger sidled up beside the boy.

'What you got kid, huh? You got somethin' for me? Wanna go shakes on it?'

The boy pushed him away. 'Fuck off, you fucking creeper.' The hand slipped from his jacket, screwdriver nestled in his fist.

The guy held up two hands. 'Take it easy kid. Hey, you come see me when you need somethin', you hear?'

Vince stopped at a rusted black door. He pushed it and found it locked, then pushed the buzzer on the intercom and it crackled.

'Yeah?'

'I'm here to see J.'

'Who is it?'

'Vince. Charlie sent me. I got some things you might be interested in.'

There was a pause, then a buzz. The door clicked. Vince pushed it open, going inside and up the stairs, the kid in his wake. On the second floor they opened a door into a room clogged with cigar smoke, a reception for some long-defunct business. A man behind the counter pointed at a door on the other side of the room. Vince nodded, crossing the room and going inside. The boy followed him in, closing the door after him.

It was a sex shop specializing in vintage and collectible memorabilia, the walls lined with glass cases and filled with every manner of oddity. The boy ran his gaze over the collection, somewhat awed and somewhat perplexed by the bounty contained therein. Vince nodded to the man and took off his backpack and set it on the counter.

'I got some stuff you might like.'

The man scratched his neck, the shirt on him tight around his heavy torso and the buttons straining to keep it together. He looked at Vincent.

'Where'd you get it, kid? I ain't into no stolen goods.'

'Some guy on the street sold me it for crack money. I'm just offering it to you.'

'Yeah? Lemme see what you got.'

Vince proceeded to empty the contents of his backpack onto the counter as the man watched, the boy watching the man. He saw an eyebrow rise as the merchandise was placed in front of him. He lifted a signed photo, turned it and placed it back on the counter.

'This from Benny Beretti's collection?'

'I don't know who that is, mister,' Vince said.

'This is Benny Beretti's stuff, you cheeky little bastard.'

'I told you, I don't know who that is. I got it off some junk–_'

'Yeah yeah, you said. Some junkie.' He paused. 'Lying prick.'

'Hey, if you don't want it…'

The man took the cigar from his mouth and flicked the ash into a stacked ashtray. 'Are you telling me if I pick up the phone and call Benny right now, he's not gonna tell me he's had his flat ransacked?'

Vince stepped forward. 'You know what, fuck it. We'll take it somewhere else.' He began to lift the things and stuff them back into his bag. The man clapped a hand on his wrist.

'Just hold on there, you little shit.' He took the VHS tape from his hand and put it down. 'I swear to Christ, you two are lying fucks, but I'll give you 150 bucks for the whole lot, take it or leave it.'

'Fuck you.' Vince proceeded to lift the stuff but the man grabbed the arm of his jacket.

'Take it or leave it, you little asshole. Because I know Benny, and he's a piece of shit, but I know him. And I could call the cops right now, 'cause I know where this stuff is from. So?'

Vince turned to look at Caleb and Caleb gave no reply, by which Vince read assent. He pushed the guy's hand away. 'Fine. Gimme the fucking money.'

The man took a fold of bills from his pocket, counted out the cash and handed it to Vince. Vince took it and stuffed it in his pocket, and picked up the backpack and slung it over his shoulder.

The boy looked into the cabinet upon which their booty lay. He caught sight of something which made him pause. He pointed at it.

'Doesn't look very vintage,' he said.

The man brushed aside the stuff and peered through the glass. He shrugged. 'Some people will pay anything to get their rocks off.'

'What is it?' the boy said.

'An operabox. Like virtual, but better.'

'How's it work?'

'How's it work? You plug yourself in, choose your show, and off you go. Take a trip. Honeys, gooks, ladyboys. Rompers. She Gung. Barbies, cockrockers. Whatever your poison.'

'How does it work? Can I try?'

'Can you try? Yeah you can try. You got two thousand bucks?'

'It costs two thousand dollars?'

The man took out a cigar and lit it. 'Look, you got your money, now go on and get the fuck outta here, stop wasting my time.' He lifted a box from the floor and hurriedly put away his new purchases. 'Go on.'

Vince took the boy by the arm. 'Come on. Let's get outta here.' He pulled him toward the door.

'Hey, you see Benny, you say hello.' The man grinned, the cigar clamped between his teeth.

They went downstairs and into the alley.

4

'I bought this for you,' he said, holding out the fine silver necklace. She blushed, taking it from him and sliding the locket through her delicate hand.

'For me?'

The boy smiled and nodded.

'How much did you pay for this?' The expression on her face was such as from one who has never owned, even held, anything of value in her life.

He shrugged. 'It doesn't matter what it cost. It's for you.'

She held it up.

'Want me to put it on?' he said.

'Okay.'

He took it from her, opening it and draping it around her neck. Her hand rose to finger the locket as he secured the clasp. The boy inhaled the scent of her hair, the heat around his neck flaring at his boldness. He sat back down. The girl looked at it once then slipped it inside her shirt.

'Thank you,' she said.

He shook his head and scratched the back of his neck in embarrassment. He turned away to look out over the city.

They were sitting on the roof of the building, seven stories up, which afforded them a dizzying view of the smog-laden city. Below them the lights of Chinatown winked through the haze. In the other direction, the hulking shell of the old stadium protruding from the bones of the city like the skeletal husk of a millennia-old, paleolithic vertebrate, the city around it the necropolis of the ages, a cascade of gaudy blinking lights and street signs the only indication of modern inhabitation. An airplane appeared overhead, a long trail in its wake. The sky purple behind it fading to a dim blue on the horizon. The girl watched the plane creep across the sky, the boy too.

'Where would you go, if you could go anywhere?' she said.

The boy shrugged. 'Dunno.'

'I'd go to Palawan.'

'Where?' The boy turned to her.

'Palawan. It's in the Philippines. It's beautiful. Wanna see?' She proceeded to dig out her phone. The boy put a hand on her arm.

'No. Don't show me. Tell me about it.'

He liked to hear her talk. She pushed the phone back in the pocket of her cargo pants and wrapped her arms around her knees.

'Palawan is very long and skinny and covered with trees from top to bottom, and all along the outside they got these lovely beaches where all the tourists come and stay, but if you wanna get away from the tourists you can go and stay in the jungle in a treehouse and eat mangoes. Mangoes grow everywhere, you can just pick them off the tree like apples, and papaya too—'

'What's papaya?'

'A big fruit like a melon. You can pick them. And in Palawan they even make curry from papaya, even though it's a fruit. Maybe mango too. You can take a boat out on the sea and eat your dinner in a boat, or you can go kayaking in the mangroves, or snorkeling. Right before breakfast every day you can go for a swim.' She paused and looked at him before turning away again. 'It's paradise.'

The boy said nothing. He looked at the thin shadow of the hills beyond the city. The limits of his world were still

28

as constricted as they were when he was a child. Then he reached down for his bag. He turned to the girl.

'I found something.'

'What?' Her hand went to her neck to play with the fine silver necklace.

He slipped his hand into the backpack. It came out holding the small device he'd found in the dead man's hand. He showed it to her.

'What is it?' She put her hand on his arm. The hair on the back of his neck bristled.

'Some kind of VR thing. You can use it to do things and go places and stuff. Maybe we can use it to go to Palawan.'

'Where'd you get it?'

'I found it. Well, I saw this guy drop it on the train. When I tried to get it back to him, he was gone. It's worth two thousand bucks.'

'Two thousand?'

'Yeah.'

She stared at it, then took it from his hand and turned it over. 'I think I've seen one of these on the internet. Isn't it…?'

He knew what she was going to say and he blushed. 'Yeah, but it's not just for that. You can use it for anything. You just need the right software.'

'Can we really go to Palawan? I mean, virtually?'

He shrugged. 'Why not…'

She smiled and handed it back to him. 'Let's go to Palawan together,' she said. She rested her head on his shoulder. The boy felt the magic flush of young love assail his bristling limbs.

When she left him that evening he took his backpack and went down from the building and out amid the city. He made his way to Eastway to the Chinese parts market known as the Big House. The Big House was five floors of computer equipment: hardware, accessories, cabling, software, hacking and cracking services, AI services, gaming, and everything between. He'd been there for games and upgrades, and to sell on a few stolen laptops, but never for the kind of thing he was now carrying in his pack. He made his way up to the fifth floor to the hardware stalls. At the back was a guy he'd punted a few stolen machines to in the past. He went in. The guy was at the counter doing business with a couple of Mexicans. The boy browsed the scant shelves of the shop while he waited. Seeing him there, the guy stuck his head out and called.

'Help ya?'

The boy looked at him and looked at the Mexicans, and stood silently and folded his arms.

'Uh-huh,' the attendant said. He turned back to the customers.

After some minutes, when the two customers had left, the boy approached the counter.

'You've been in here before,' the guy said. The boy nodded. 'You selling?'

The boy shook his head and took the operabox from the pack and laid it on the counter.

'Jesus Christ.' The guy picked it up and turned it over. 'Where'd you get your hands on this?'

'Found it,' the boy said.

He grinned. 'Found it, did ya? And what are you looking for?'

'You got any cards for it?'

'Kid, if we sold this stuff here the law would never be outta here. We don't touch this stuff. Nobody here does.'

'Where can I find someone who does?'

'Shit, you go down any alley around here and there'll be some schmuck'll sell you cards for this, but you need to be careful. This shit gets scary pretty quickly.'

'What do you mean?'

'What he means is…' The boy looked up to see a man standing next to him, tattoos up his arms to the shoulder and a silver earring in one ear. '…this isn't somethin' gamerboys wanna be messin' around with. This shit'll take you down the

30

rabbit hole, know what I mean pal?'

The man had a weird accent.

'I just wanna use it for travel,' the boy said.

The man with the tattoos laughed. 'Do you now? Aye well, there's a million ways to travel, my friend. Not all of them legal.'

'I want to go to Palawan.'

'I have no idea what the fuck Palawan is, partner, but if it's travelin' you want, maybe you come and see me then.'

The man looked at the guy behind the counter to make sure he wasn't stepping on any toes. Then he took a card from his pocket and handed it to the boy.

'You come and see me anytime.' The boy looked at the card. Some address in Chinatown. 'But not before twelve, you hear me? My nights are long and full of horror.'

He grinned. The boy slipped the card in his pocket and nodded. 'Thanks.'

'No problem kid.'

The boy turned and left.

The next day, Saturday, the boy made his way through Chinatown right after twelve. The place was buzzing and full of hustle but the boy's mind was elsewhere. He thought of his mother, who'd been knocking on his door late morning. He recalled her offer. She'd wanted to spend time with him. The guilt tore at him and clawed at his mind as he marched on, head to the ground, shoulders hunched in a kind of torturous lurch. Maybe he'd do something for her. Maybe he'd buy her something. She would like that. And it would make him feel better. Resolved, he marched on. He stopped at a Chinese medicine store and showed the man there the card. The man pointed toward the fish market.

'In there?' the boy said.

'Other side.'

The boy nodded and went on, cutting through the fish market, stopping at a stall where an enormous catfish head sat, the mouth opening and closing mechanically despite the absence of a body. The boy stared at it in awe, wondering what strange magic was the cause of it. The fishhead stared blankly from the silver tray on which it sat, the barbels on it twitching. The boy looked at the man behind the stall like he were some kind of mage. Then he turned and walked away.

On the other side of the fish market, next to a launderette, the boy found the address scrawled on the card. He battered on the aluminum door to no avail, and waiting for some moments, hammered on it again. When he was sure he'd been given the wrong address, he turned to go. The door opened, and the boy turned to see the man with the tattoos. The man scratched his face and rubbed the back of his neck.

'Jesus Christ, pal,' he said, flexing his neck. The boy held up the card. 'Aye. When I said twelve, I didn't mean twelve. Fuck sake. Come in.'

The man turned and wandered back down the stairs. The boy followed. When they came into the room below, the boy stopped still, staring at the circle of chairs and the wires and the screens.

'What is this place?' he said.

'You needn't concern yourself with this stuff, pal. Through here.' The man gestured through a door and the boy entered. The room inside, once a kitchen, was strewn with electronics of every kind: on the table, on the counter, on the chairs and on the floor. The man turned on a coffee machine and yawned. 'Haven't even had my coffee yet. Cunts knockin' on my door and it's not even lunchtime.'

He sat at a counter while the coffee brewed. He brushed aside an assortment of chips and boards with his arm and flicked a hand. 'Right. Come on, show us what you got.'

The boy took off his pack and laid it on the counter, and took out the operabox and handed it to the man.

'I just want software,' he said.

The man looked at the kit and raised an eyebrow. 'Oh aye? You got an epidural, have ya?'

'A what?' The boy frowned.

'Epidural. The kit's no good without an epidural.' He placed it on the counter. 'You have no idea what you have here, do ya?'

The boy reached out to lift the box and the man held up his hands. 'Hey, do what you like. I'm just tryin' to help, kid.'

The boy lifted the operabox and turned it over, and looked back at the man. 'Do you have an epidural?'

He nodded. 'I can sell you one, aye. They don't come cheap. But you can't use the box without one.'

'How much?'

He shrugged. 'I can do you an old wired one for 75 bucks. Sterilized, of course. Nothing to worry about. Still works a treat.'

'And the software?'

'What were you lookin'?'

'I need a card for Palawan.'

'Palawan? Fuck's Palawan?' He stood up and turned to the coffee machine and poured a cup.

'It's an island in the Philippines.'

The man put down the coffee, reached up into the cupboard and pulled down a tin. He put it on the counter, sat and opened it. 'Fucking Palawan. I got Patpong, if ya like. That's a popular one. Or Phuket...'

'I want Palawan.'

'What about some Deadhead? A young kid like you, it's all the rage. Or Wingnuts, or—'

'I want Palawan.'

The man glanced at him. 'Fuck sake.' He rifled through the box, pulling out micro-SD cards in small packets. 'Look kid, I got the Seychelles here, but it's dull as fuck, I assure ya. Or here ya go – Bali. Close enough, innit?'

'It's not what I'm looking for. I need Palawan.'

The man sighed. 'Not worth the fuckin' trouble,' he muttered, then took a sip of his coffee. 'Tell ya what, you take Bali and give it a shot. And if ya like it, I'll build you a custom trip for this fuckin' Palawan, alright?' He tossed the card across the counter. 'But it'll cost ya. For the pure fuckin' boredom it's gonna cost me, ya hear? I gotta make these dull-as-fuck tourist trips up frame by frame, and it bores the piss clean outta me.' He put the lid back on the box. 'Fuckin' Palawan...'

'How much is this?' the boy said.

'You can have it.' The man took a sip of his coffee and stood up. 'If ya promise not to come here breakin' my balls before lunch again, ya hear me?'

He stood up. 'Come on. Let's get you an epidural.'

He led him back out into the hive room to the far wall where he opened a panel in the wall and took out another box.

'I keep these around, ya know, just in case I run out of disposables. Folk don't want the old wired ones anymore. Don't suppose you give a fuck though, do ya?'

He took an epidural out, the thing sealed in a plastic wrapper. 'I sterilize these after each use, then seal them up for the next time. People get freaky about this kinda thing, and I'm never done explainin' it to them. They're clean, alright?' He held it out to the boy.

The boy took it from him and looked at it. 'What do you do with it?'

The man shook his head. 'Totally green, aren't ya?' He took the epidural from the boy and ripped open the packet. 'Come over here.'

He sat down on a chair and pulled up another for the boy. 'Gimme the box. And the card.'

The boy handed him the operabox and the man plugged in the epidural and told the boy to turn around.

'Why?'

'Why? So I can show you how to use the fuckin' thing. I'm not gonna touch you up, for fuck's sake. Turn around.'

The boy spun the revolving chair around. The man held the plug out in front of the boy's face. 'See these pins?'

The boy nodded.

'They go in the back of your neck. And once they're in, you pull this little lever here. That'll hold them in. Got it?'

'Yeah.'

'Now, it hurts when it goes in, so I'm gonna demonstrate for ya.'

He placed the plug on the back of the boy's neck and pushed in until it was buried in the boy's skin. The boy hissed. Then the man flicked the switch and the boy cried out with pain as the micro-barbs lodged in his skin.

'Telt ye. That's why people like the disposable these days – no pain, and cleaner.'

'How much are the disposable?' the boy said.

'Can't do them for less than 250 a pop. Hard to come by, they are. And getting harder.'

The man spun the boy's chair around and held up the box. 'Now, it's important you put the epidural in before you turn on the box, ya got me? And once the plug's in, you put your card in here…'

Noticing a card already in the device, the man popped it out. He turned it over in his hand. 'Already a card in here, kid. Was this in it when you got it?'

The boy nodded.

'Wanna give me it? I love a good mystery card, me. I'll give you the epidural buckshee.'

'Huh?'

'Free, pal. You can have the epidural for the card.'

The boy reached out and took it from the man. 'It's not for sale.'

He sighed. 'Fine.' He stood up. 'Have a toy around with gettin' the epidural out yourself. It's 75 for the plug. You break the pins on it, you buy a new one. I don't do repairs. And no warranties on this shit.'

The boy took out his cash and counted out the money and handed it to the man.

'Ta. And pal, if you don't know what's on that other card, I suggest you don't plug into it. Not your first time, at least.

There's some fucked-up trips out there, custom jobs for sick fucks, ken what I mean?'

The boy wasn't sure he did, but he nodded.

'Aye. Watch yourself.'

5

When he got home later he found the apartment empty. His mother was gone and had left a pizza on the kitchen table with a note that said she'd been asked to work and would be back late. The boy felt fresh pangs of guilt, realizing he'd neglected to buy her something. He groaned and clenched his fists, and went to the bedroom and took off his shoes and his backpack and went back to the kitchen. After he'd eaten some pizza he messaged the girl.

Wanna hang out?

It was some time before she got back and when she did she told him she was out with friends and maybe she'd see him later that evening. He put the phone down on the kitchen table and went to his room and lay on the bed.

When he woke it was dark. He sat up and looked out the window to see the familiar lights. His mind went to the operabox. He took it from his bag and looked at it, then plugged it into the wall the check the charge. He took the micro-SD he'd bought from the bag and opened the small packet and let it slip out into his hand. He looked at it with disappointment, as if he'd expected the exterior to somehow hint at what worlds the card might contain. He put it on the dresser.

In the kitchen he checked his phone. The girl hadn't

messaged. He went back to the bedroom and locked the door, and took out the epidural and plugged it into the box. He popped out the SD that was in the machine and looked at it. The same, it told no stories, gave no clue what was contained therein. His breathing quickened. He picked up the Bali card and looked at it once more. He could... But it was for the girl. It was a gift for her, and he wanted her to see it first. He put it down again and reinserted the other. He took a deep breath, his eyes closing, then put down the box and lifted the epidural. Hesitating a second, he reached behind him and plugged it into his neck. He winced, water coming to his eye. Then he lay down on the bed. The machine lay small and snug in his hand, gateway to a thousand worlds. He turned it on, and was almost disappointed when he saw the dated LCD display. He scrolled down through the menu; it was much like a video game, showing 'OPTIONS' and 'CONTROLS' and 'MUSIC' and so on. These he skipped, and went straight to 'PLAY'. His finger hovered over the button for a few moments. Then he pushed it. A warning flashed on the small screen:

You are about to enter the mindscape. What follows is an entirely mental journey and is not real...

He scrolled down through the disclaimer and when he reached the bottom, hit 'ACCEPT'. An alien tingling sensation assailed the back of his neck and crept up into his head, and then—

A stabbing electrical pain, then it was over. He opened his eyes. His room was gone. A white rain falling around him. A sensation like flying, or rather the 'world' flying at him then coming to a halt, and he sitting in a taxi frozen in time. Then it was as if someone hit the 'PLAY' button, and the taxi came to life, the radio playing, the driver turning to look out the window at a guy playing saxophone on the sidewalk, the blare of a horn behind them. The taxi pulled up to the curb and came to a standstill. The driver turned, draping an arm over the seat.

'You're here.'

The boy looked down at his bag and began to shove a hand into his pocket, but the driver held up a hand.

'Ride's on us. Get outta here.'

The boy looked at the driver. He looked familiar, but in an unplaceable kinda way.

'Thanks,' the boy said. He got out of the taxi.

His feet on the asphalt, he stopped and looked around him. It was nowhere he recognized but he did not feel lost. He felt like he knew exactly where he was going. He felt an unusual vigor. The ground underfoot was pleasing and the sky above him blue, impossibly blue, and all around him the world had a kind of intensity of color and sound he'd never seen before. He walked toward the building in front of him, which by its exterior looked like a library. Maybe a bank. Two large Doric columns spanned the tiny door, and when he reached it an old man sitting at the foot of one of the columns held out a hand.

'This is the last time I'm gonna ask,' the old man said.

The man was in tattered clothes, a cap on his head and a walking stick laying across his lap.

The boy stupidly put a hand in his pocket and fished out nothing. 'I don't have nothin', mister.'

'I knew your father,' the man said.

'What?'

'And your whore mother.' The old man grinned and his tongue shot lewdly from his mouth to lick his upper lip.

'Who the fuck are you?' the boy said.

'New here, kid?'

The boy turned away.

'Matricide or necrophilia, what's your poison?'

'Fuck you, old man.'

The old man's laughter grated on him as he walked away. When he reached the door of the building, he opened it and stepped inside.

A man in a yellow suit sat at a desk, in front of him a piece of paper and a pencil. He sat cross-legged like an ancient raconteur, a cigarette between his yellowed fingers. He cleared his throat and flicked the ash from the cigarette heedlessly as the boy stopped at the desk.

'We presume you're familiar with our disclaimer policy, because we know you sat and read every word of it, right?' The man winked, then his demeanor became serious again. 'We have a hard copy of your assent to our terms and conditions, so put your winding scrawl here so's there's no misunderstandings later. You know, should you kill yourself.'

The boy looked at him. 'You want my name?'

'Your *signature.*' He took an elaborate puff of his cigarette.

The boy picked up the pencil and scribbled illegibly on the paper.

'Very well.' The man sat back and regarded him.

The boy hesitated. 'Is that it?'

The man nodded long and slow. When the boy turned to go, the man said, 'How would you do it, just out of interest?'

The boy stopped. 'Do what?'

'Kill yourself.'

'How would I kill myself?'

'Momma's pills? Bedsheet on the back of the door? Stanley knife in the bath?' The boy was about to hurry away when the man waved a finger. 'Nah… I know, you cheeky little bastard. You're a jumper. Seventh floor right to the ground – do not pass "Go". Hah? Yeah, I see you…'

As the boy pushed the door open, the man had a final word:

'Better men than you have decamped rashly this mortal coil.'

He was spitting cigarette smoke into the air as the boy stepped inside. The door closed behind him and the room, which was entirely dark, turned silver, like the inside of a highly polished orb. When he turned, he saw the door was no longer there. In the middle of the room, curving away to nothing, was a giant hole like a reservoir overflow drain. The boy could not see into it, but he could feel it, feel the weight of its gravity, its emptiness. A cold and hollow nothingness that descended into the pit of his very being. Like the end of everything. As he felt the tug of this hole of insanity pulling at him and threatening to engulf him, a table materialized on his left, and then another. At the first sat a huge woman with one gross leg planted on the table, opposite her a man who was eating cataracted eyes from between her toes. The boy felt a wave of revulsion and looked away. At the other table, a man cutting off his fingers one after the other for the amusement of three men who watched with glee. Music rose. A bizarre and grotesque carnivalesque jazz. More tables popped up and soon the room was a crowded heaving thing, a living thing but with all the weight of the earth's dead. The boy looked over his shoulder again; the door was still gone. He turned and crossed the room. He passed a man putting a needle through his tongue, the mouth already full with needles and in his lips and cheeks, and a woman with a monstrous parasitic baby chewing through her bleeding nipples. A table of whores saw him hurry by and pulled him in. 'A fresh one!' one cried and jumped up on the table and opened her legs. Her friend dragged the boy to her and held out his hand and the one on the table took it and fed it inside her sex. It took the hand, then the arm – 'What the hell? Let me go!' – then the boy was up to the elbow inside her and the cunt like the mouth of a viper still swallowing his arm like an undigested lunch. 'Get the fuck off me!' The arm up to the shoulder now and the boy screaming. The whores in laughter and ribald, and one starts chewing on the flesh of her forearm. Vampire cunts. The boy's shoulder about to pop, when he's grabbed around the ankles by an enormous circus performer in a leotard and hauled out. In his bloodied hand is a miscarried child. He drops it to the floor with a spatter and stumbles back, falls at the feet of the man who laughs and hoists him to his feet. 'How do I get outta here, tell me how to get out…' The man doesn't answer but takes the cigar from his mouth and puts it out in his own eye. 'Jesus, get me outta here…' The boy turns and stumbles again, feeling the galactic weight of that swirling black hole in the middle of the room, feels its pull, and that is not where he wants to be, he only wants out, out and into the air and free. The room tilts and the boy feels he's in a kind of landslide, but he's the only one dragged by it, everyone around him in their blind orgy of violence and oblivious, and he slides toward the middle of the room, two human heads rolling past him, eyes wide in mirth, silver teeth in their mouths; the boy grabs a table leg as he nears the center of the room, clings to it, the weight of that hole more than all life could bear. The room rights itself, the silver walls of the vast ballroom turning a malevolent blue before turning silver again. The boy stands up and a man puts an arm around him, an old man, a kindly man, he raises his hat to greet the boy and inside the hollow of his head is a huge nesting crow eating its young. The boy screams a silent scream and pulls away. An old sow with a toothless smile lifts a withered breast and slices it off, and holds it out to him. *Scream. Don't run. Don't show fear. This place is your fear. Fight your fear.* A woman like a mother takes his hand as he spins about in terror and pulls him into her lap. 'Child, be with me,' she says, and she takes his hand and pulls it into her bosom. The boy breathes. The boy feels safe. She strokes his face. She licks his wet eyes. She sucks his nose, puts her tongue up a nostril. 'There there now,' she whispers, and when the boy drifts into a nothing sleep she tilts his head and puts her tongue in his ear, and the boy hears a holy evil drip into him like treacle: *a man on fire gives birth to the children of night and in the bloody aftermath of their birth they drank the blood that was nectar of the Cathar and Merovingian line, queens bold and queens incestuous, and from their loins the torch of dying equivocation whose virtue was like salt in the dying wound, hear me child for these are the words of the raging mother* – mother – *cunt of all life, a vast and vacuous waste her womb but filled with treasures all – hear her rattle when she moves? shake her and emeralds fall from her pores, eat one and feel the barbed prick of antiquity in the empty halls of your bones* – the emptiness in the boy growing, the vast and unencumbrable hole of everything

42

swallowing him, and outside his being the hole pulling him to it, but within and without only one hole threatening to meet itself in the middle and ingurgitate all – *hear, child, the sisters of eternal lore, the deathlore, the signs and treaties of their stigmata tales the last a man hears before the groan of the allseeing whore, a terrible deathrattle and within it the demise of the farshore of hope, seething, boy, is the sea that has brought you here, and seething the sea which you must cross to take you home, but only listen to your cuntmother and hear the strings of silence that she pours into you lullabyshy like the first gargles of her cursed womb* – the boy engulfed, the hole upon him, he opened his eyes and bit the tongue which emptied the ancient augments into his ear, and the woman bleeding from the mouth pushed him off her knee and to the floor. A thousand whores kicked and bit him, and tore at his clothes, and he crawled under their stamping feet, his face bloody and scratched and the howls of wickedness in his ear. He saw a light. A tumultuous light. He fled under their skirts and boots toward that light. And emerging from the dark tunnel of their savagery he saw a man in silver seated at an altar of sorts and he fled toward it, throwing himself at his feet. The whores retreated and their chatter died, and the silver-sheen of the iniquitous ballroom turned a deep scarlet. The man all in silver raised the boy to his feet and took his head in his hands and stared into his eyes and kissed him on the lips. 'You want to leave, yes?' The boy cried, tears in his eyes: 'Yes!' 'Then I shall let you leave. Here, perceive and behold your end,' and into the boy poured a golddark light that the boy knew as the map of his earthly travails—

my mother died when she birthed me and my father burned her corpse. the savage nurses of castaway children fed me the acrid poison of fell teets until my babymouth rotted and rot grew there, and the taste of rot would be known every time the baby opened his mouth to beg for sustenance, and the nurses heard it and knew the sound of this foul rot and so denied the child food. the baby was born and the child died. the child lived and spurned love, and the nurses took what they were owed. angels died when they heard the vicious child. the child died a hundred times and never cried. the child was a killer and killed his sister in the womb. his sister was reborn and never knew the thirst for vengeance. the child was the progeny of rape. his mother begged for rape and got it. the mother took revenge on the body of the child, her body feeding the growing fetus on the detritus of her body, the bile and the fat and the poisonous airs. the child born slug. a slug child. pour salt on the slugchild and hear it peal. let it run liquid fat then light it on fire. the child had a grandfather who hung himself. the grandmother found the body of the grandfather and shot herself in the mouth with a rifle. see, child, the things you have spawned? *i see*. see how reviled you are? *i see*. what did your mother do? *she bit off my organs and fed them to the neighbor's child*. and what did your father do? *my father spat on my bed and called me filth*. and what did your sister do? *my sister forgave me*. and what, child, are you? *i am all-hated*. Tell me again. *i am hated among all*. more. *i am filth, filthchild, forebear and kin of all the children of pollution and all the dirtscraps of miscarried castoffs*. you are swine. *i am. kill me. kill me! let me fucking die, kill me, fucking kill me—*

The hole that consumed consumed. The boy let himself be taken. When the room tilted again, the boy let go and slid toward the center of the gaping jaws, and in him the words of the silver man opening a greater hole yet, and the two holes coming together rent apart and merged at once, and for once and for all the boy was free. Darkness took him.

6

He opened his eyes and saw the dull light of a polluted sky and thought he was dead. Then a face like his. A boy's. He reached up to touch the hovering face as if to check it was real. The stranger took his hand gently and placed it on his chest. Caleb was trembling.

'Where am I?' he whispered.

'On the roof.'

'What am I doing here?'

The stranger held up the operabox. 'You were wearing this.'

Caleb began to cry. He curled up in a ball and covered his face. The other boy sat down on the ground and watched him. It was some minutes before he stopped.

'What happened to you?' the stranger said.

Caleb sat up. 'I think I met the devil,' he whispered.

'With this?'

Caleb nodded.

The stranger stood up and walked to look out over the city and to the street below. Caleb glanced up at him and an instant pang of recognition hit him.

'I saw you... before, I mean. I saw you on the roofs...'

The stranger didn't say anything.

'Who are you?'

He turned to Caleb and held out a hand. When the boy extended his, the stranger pulled Caleb to his feet. 'My name is Saleh.'

'What are you doing up here?'

Saleh shrugged. 'I like it. I spend all my time up here.'

'And you found me lying here?'

'I found you standing there.' Saleh pointed to the ledge.

Caleb leaned out to look. He was on the top of his building. It was seven floors to the tarmac below. 'You mean, I was—?'

Saleh nodded. 'You were going to jump, yes.'

The boy closed his eyes.

'Is it because of this?'

Caleb looked at him and the operabox Saleh was holding in his hand, and slowly and with hesitation he held out his hand and Saleh placed it into his palm. He nodded.

'You saw the devil and he told you to jump?'

The boy shook his head. 'I saw... terrible things.'

'Maybe you shouldn't use that thing. I know what it is, what they're for. People use it for bad things. People die using it you know.'

The boy pushed it deep into the pocket of his cargo pants. 'I never want to see that again.'

Saleh turned and sat on the edge of the building and sat quietly and looked out at the ravaged city. The boy shivered. He felt suddenly cold and folded his arms. He sat next to Saleh. When he looked to the ground far below, a thing that had never before troubled him: he felt a dread that almost crippled his soul. He emitted a kind of crushed groan.

'Maybe you should go down,' Saleh said.

The boy shook his head. 'I'm fine.'

Saleh nodded. Caleb looked out over the vista.

'You live around here?' he asked.

'Back there,' Saleh said, indicating over his shoulder with the flick of a hand.

'You live alone?'

'I got people.'

They fell silent for a bit. Caleb noticed the thin sweat on his body had turned cold. There was a dull pain in the center of his mind and the point where the epidural had punctured the back of his neck stung. He raised a hand to touch it.

'Where did you get that thing?' Saleh said.

'I found it.'

Saleh snorted. 'You mean you stole it.'

'Kinda.'

'It's expensive, you know.'

The boy nodded. 'Yeah, I heard.'

'You could sell it.'

The boy was quiet for a moment, then he said, 'I wanted to do something for someone.'

Saleh said nothing. Caleb felt heat creep up his face from his neck and he said no more. He quickly changed the subject.

'What do you do up here?'

Saleh became suddenly animated and gave a hearty shrug. 'I run, jump, find new corners of the city. It's my world up here. Sometimes you bump into a few old men feeding pigeons or a crazy old woman with her bees, but usually there's no one. It's only me. This is where I feel free. Totally free.'

Caleb looked at Saleh and saw a kind of glowing wonder on his face. He was intrigued.

'Wanna come down and eat something?' he said.

Saleh's eyes narrowed. 'You live here?'

'Yeah, down there. Third floor.'

'You live alone?'

The boy shook his head. 'Nah, with my mom. But she's at work.'

Saleh shrugged. 'Sure. Okay.'

Caleb stood up and turned.

'How'd you get up here?' Saleh said. 'The roof door's locked.'

The boy pointed at the other side of the building. 'The quickest way.'

Saleh grinned and followed him over to the wall and they

both looked down at the series of balconies and downspouts that would take them to the third floor.

'I think we'll get along,' Saleh said.

Caleb grinned and threw one leg over the side, and took hold of the downspout, something he'd done a hundred times before. This time he was assailed by a fear he'd never known. He blocked out the thick terror in his belly and the horrid metallic tang in his mouth and shimmied down to the balcony below.

The boy took easily to life above the city. Nights they roamed free, over the city's vast gloaming, over the rooftops of warehouse and domicile, offices and derelict buildings, running, leaping, creeping and swinging. Saleh was simian-like in his acclimatization to height, and Caleb, no stranger to the more unreachable parts of the city, learned quickly under Saleh's schooling. The boy began to map out the city in his head to an extent he'd never before dreamed of, even in all his childhood wanderings when his imagination, inspired by the lights of the city, sent him on journeys into the dark magic of unknown corners where adventure lurked. Now those adventures became reality and were enacted nightly on the crests and summits of that twilight world. Saleh took him for the first time onto the roof of the Chinese Theater, where they crawled inside, into the attic, and found themselves in the cavernous halls of that veiled place, the stage dark, the stalls quiet, and the sets for the plays sitting about in disarray, casting strange oriental shadows about the place. Silhouettes, caricatures, lions, dragons, painted coolied peasants in a procession across the stage. Shadowfolk hiding in all corners, witness to the boys' intrusion.

'How often do you come here?' the boy whispered.

'I only been once,' Saleh said.

They found the back room of the theater where costumes were piled high in bursting boxes, props scattered over table and floor. Caleb found a long oriental pipe, an opium pipe, silver and jade and exquisitely carved. He put it in his mouth to puff on it and made Saleh laugh. By the time he took it from his mouth he'd become irrevocably attached to it and put it in his backpack.

'I don't steal,' Saleh said.

'It's just a souvenir.'

Saleh turned away. But in the dressing room they found a picture of a woman taped to a mirror, a bewitching Asiatic face painted white and with the look of long ages in her eyes. The picture looked as from a time long passed.

'Who do you think she is?' Saleh said.

The boy shrugged. 'Dunno. Whoever she is, she's dead now.'

When the boy turned to leave, Saleh snatched the picture from the mirror and pushed it into his pocket.

They crept up into the eaves to look out over the theater from above.

'Did you see a show when you came before?' the boy asked.

'No.'

'Next time we come, let's see a show.'

'Okay.'

They left, going back onto the roof to look down at the hive streets of Chinatown. Oblivious, those below, to the pair on the rooftops that watched eagle-eyed from silhouettes of the upper regions of the city. Perhaps too there were eyes that watched, unseen, and tracked their night-wanderings. Two shadows pursued by shadows. Night martens, roof whisperers, the vigilant and the sleepless. A shadow theater that played out against the crepuscular hues of the night sky.

'Wanna see my favorite place in the city?'

Caleb nodded. 'Where is it?'

'Come on.'

They ran, crept, swung, and leapt across Chinatown and over the Beltway and into the business district, where behind the Old Mercantile Bank building Saleh took him up the side of a five-story office block and onto the roof, and right there in the center of the roof was a shrine, a small temple of sorts, an island sacristy in the vast sky of a looming metropolis.

'What is it?'

Saleh grinned. 'I'll show you. Come on in. Don't make any sudden movements.'

Saleh led him to the door, put his hand on the handle, and before opening turned to the boy and warned him with a gesture of the hand to go slowly. Then he opened the door and stepped in, the boy going after. Inside, a monkey reclining on a majlis sofa leapt up and screeched. Caleb recoiled, but the monkey, recognizing Saleh, relaxed, and stepped down off the sofa and held out a hand with an affable howl.

'It knows you?' the boy said, stepping back and staring at his friend.

'Yeah. I come here all the time.'

Then the monkey flickered like a glitchy rendering before clarity resumed.

'It's virtual?' the boy said incredulously.

Saleh laughed. 'Of course it is. Who would lock up a real monkey on the roof of a building?'

The monkey gestured Saleh to the sofa. The boy watched as Saleh and the monkey sat side by side. Saleh looked up at him and grinned. 'Watch this.' He reached into his pocket and took out a candy bar and held it out. The monkey screeched and reached a hand inside a small pouch on its waist and too out a silver coin, holding it out to Saleh. Saleh reached out to take it and his hand slipped right through the mirage. The monkey howled.

'What the hell?' the boy said.

'It's a virtual Hanuman.'

'A what?'

'Hanuman. Some rich white guy married a Hindu woman and decided to convert, and he thought it'd be a good idea to build a shrine to Hanuman and stick a virtual monkey in it. Idiot.'

The boy put his hands in his pockets and stared at the

monkey. 'It looks so real.' He looked around. The walls were covered with Hindu devotional pictures and yantras. In the center of the wall, a giant picture of the monkey god, a crown on his head and a golden scepter cradled in his arm. The smell of incense in the place was making him nauseous.

'Let's get outta here,' he said. 'This place is weird.'

'Fine.' Saleh stood up. He turned and offered his hand to the monkey, and the simian reached out to shake, a virtual hand slipping through Saleh's. The monkey cackled. It followed the boys to the door, watching as they went back out into the night. It was grunting at them as Saleh closed the door.

'Too weird,' the boy said as they crossed the roof. 'Who the hell keeps a virtual monkey?'

'There are worse things you can do with your money.'

Saleh climbed out onto the ledge.

The girl texted him, asking him where he'd been. Said she hadn't seen him. He told her to come up to the apartment later that evening. His mom would be out. The boy went to the drawer where he'd hidden the operabox and took it out. He hadn't touched it since that night. He sat down on the bed and turned it over in his hand, then he pushed out the SD card that was nestled in the side of the device. He shuddered, a cold sweat breaking out on the back of his neck. He stood up and went to the balcony. The card in his hand had a peculiar weight to it, more than was merited by its tiny size and flimsy makeup. He tried to muster the will to fling it into the night, but the will was not in him and he went back inside and took the opium pipe that now sat on his shelf, and unscrewing the silver mouthpiece inserted the card into the body of the pipe and reassembled it. He returned the pipe to the shelf.

The other card did not have the same ominous weight. The other card did not fill him with the same dread. Still, he put the card in the machine with trepidation and it clicked into place, and when he sat down on the bed to put the epidural in his neck his hand was shaking. The boy raised the plug, and thinking only of the girl, pushed it into his skin. Then he lay back and switched on the box.

When he awoke from his reverie, he felt out of his own body. The room around him felt unreal, as if he'd awoken from true reality and found it wanting, found that it lacked the same visceral tangibility as that from which he'd just awoken. He felt empty and longed to return. Then the smell of gravy hit him and made him feel ill. He pulled the epidural from his neck and sat up, listening for noises from the kitchen. His mom was home. He pushed the operabox under the duvet of his bed and got up and went out. Hearing him come in, she turned and smiled.

'Hey. I called you but you must have been sleeping. You hungry?'

'I thought you were working.'

'I am. I just came home to eat.'

He looked around furtively. 'What time you going out again?'

His mom let off stirring the gravy. 'You trying to get rid of me?'

'What? No.' He hovered about the table.

'Sit down. We'll eat together.'

The boy sat down.

'Almost ready.'

The boy sat quietly while his mom related her day, her trials and labors. When she was done cooking, she put a plate in front of him.

'I bought the chicken in the deli on the way back. The Italian one. You always liked their chicken.'

'Thanks Mom.'

She was about to sit down when the doorbell rang. The boy jumped up. 'I'll get it.'

The girl was at the door and smiled when he opened. He beckoned her in.

'Hey.'

'Hey.' Her smile made him feel shy.

She smelled the food. 'Is your mom here?'

He nodded. 'Yeah.' He gestured inside.

When he got to the kitchen door, he hovered there uncertainly. His mom stood up from the table.

'Hey Aurora.' She gestured to the table. 'Don't just stand there, come in and sit down. Let me get you something to eat…'

'No, it's fine, really…'

'Don't be silly. Sit down.'

They sat down and his mom prepared another plate for the girl and joined them at the table. She rode out the awkward silence before saying, 'This is nice, isn't it? Nice to have some company, I mean. Sometimes it feels like I don't even have a son.'

Caleb shot his mother a reproachful look.

'Well, you never come out of your room, do you? You're like a hermit. I don't know what you do in there all day and night. Maybe you can tease him out into the light, Aurora.'

The girl smiled.

'Well, don't just sit there. Eat.'

They ate. Soon they loosened up and the girl told the boy's mom about school and what she was doing, and the boy's mom even joked that Caleb might go back if she spoke to the principal and he said sorry about what he'd done, but his silence soon put an end to her prompting. Aurora told her she was building a paper theater for an expo and told her about the little play she'd written, and how she'd perform it at the end of the year. The boy was mostly silent as he ate, only rising from his food now and again to sneak a glance at the girl as she chatted animatedly to his mother.

When they finished eating, he was quick to get up from the table.

'Wanna go hang out?'

The girl nodded and smiled, and thanked his mom for the dinner. Aurora lifted her plate, and his mom reached out to take it from her.

'Really, Ms. Linz, you don't have to…'

When the boy's mom tried to take the plate, the sleeves of the girl's top rode up her forearm, exposing the bruises there. They both looked down at her arms. The girl turned pale.

'Aurora… are you alright?'

'What? Oh no, it's nothing. I'm fine…'

She turned away and hurried out of the kitchen, and sharing a glance with his mother, a glance that spoke much, the boy turned and followed Aurora into the bedroom. He shut the door.

'Are you—?'

'I'm fine.'

He said no more, but sat down on the bed. She sat beside him. They sat in silence until he slid his hand under the duvet and took out the device and showed it to her. She looked up at him, eyes wide with intrigue.

'I got you something…'

'Palawan?' Her voice quivered. She put a hand on his arm.

'Uhm, it's Bali, but the man said if you liked it he'd make up a special one for you, and I'd buy it for you and everything…'

He pretended not to see the disappointment that flashed in her eyes.

'Wanna try?'

She smiled. 'Yeah. Okay.'

He took the epidural and with a softwipe he cleaned it and dried it off, then he gave the epidural to the girl and told her where to put it.

'Can't you do it?'

'I don't want to hurt you.'

'You won't…'

'It's painful.'

'Try it.'

He pulled down the neck of her sweater and put it to her neck, and gently as he could, pushed until it buried itself in her skin. She didn't make a sound, even if a tear appeared in her eye. Then he told her to lie down and she did, and he placed the device into her hand.

'Can't we go together?' she said.

'I only have one thing,' he said, pointing at the epidural.

'Oh.'

'Hit play when you're ready.'

'Will it hurt?'

He shook his head. Somewhere in the back of his mind, recollections of the trip to the hell-place assailed him.

She looked up at him before lowering her gaze to the LCD screen of the device. Then she hit play and closed her eyes.

He watched her. He'd no idea for how long, but he watched, noting, subconsciously perhaps, the changes in the micro-expressions on her face and the twitches, and the tiny smile that upturned the corners of her face and the eyes that smiled even though they were closed, and the countenance of her face turned so that the boy thought she was the most beautiful creature he'd ever seen and it made him want to weep.

When she finally awoke from the dream of Bali, she sat up and the boy sat next to her and she took his face in her hands and kissed him, and when he opened his eyes there were tears running down her face.

'I want to go away from here and never come back,' she said.

7

'I need to make money. A lot of it.'

Saleh turned to look at him. They were in the Barrio district, perched atop the medical wing of the university, which teetered above a vast, ill-lit green expanse below. They watched the bicycle lights of night couriers crossing the park, laden with whatever contraband they ferried through the dusk. Saleh kicked his legs idly.

'I told you, I don't steal.'

'Do you know anywhere where *I* can steal?'

Saleh shook his head. The boy turned to look out into the night. 'I wanna go away.'

'Where?'

'The Philippines.'

Saleh scrutinized him with his dark eyes. 'Are you in love?'

The boy blushed and lowered his eyes. 'No.'

'But there's a girl, isn't there.'

He was quiet for a moment. 'How did you know?'

'Because you're talking crazy.'

The hum of a police helicopter could be heard in the distance.

'This place is crazy,' the boy said.

'Yes.' Saleh sighed. 'But so is everywhere.'

They watched as the helicopter became visible and came

to a rest, hovering over the far end of the park, an eye in the sky, the watcher in the clouds. All over the park, the bicycle lights went dark.

Saleh stood up. 'Come on, let's get out of here. We don't want to get spotted.'

On his way home that night, the boy stopped at the girl's balcony to have a look in the window. A torturous guilt assailed him as he dropped down onto her balcony, and he promised himself this would be the last time he'd spy on her. She'd kissed him. Maybe she loved him too. From here on, he'd respect her and not do anything that might jeopardize that.

When he stretched up to the window, she was at the mirror in the bathroom, staring at herself, a lost look on her face. Vulnerable and small, without her smile, her smile that destroyed him a little every time he saw it. Horrified at his intrusion, yet he could not pull himself away from the window. He stared at her troubled figure and his heart broke. He resolved to save her. To take her away from it all to a place where she might close her eyes and smile the way she had when she'd lain on his bed. A place to forget. He would be the one to save her, and she would love him for it forever.

He watched the girl reach behind her neck and unclasp the locket he'd given her. She held it in her hand and looked at it for what seemed to him a long time, and when she touched it with her finger he blinked away a tear that came to his eye. She laid the locket on the sink and opened the little glass mirror in front of her, taking out some cleaning wipes and closing it again. She took one out and began to wipe her face. That face. The face of an angel.

When she jerked her head to the door, an alarm tugged at his heart. He saw the instinctive defensiveness in her posture, like an animal cornered. He couldn't hear, but he knew her father was on the other side of the door. The girl put a hand on the sink. When the father banged on the door again, the boy heard it. Heard the insistence in the pounding. Then heard him shout. The girl went to the door and put a hand on the handle, and jumped when there was another thump. The boy too. When the girl was forced to open the door, the father pushed his way inside, Aurora backing up until she was at the sink and she could retreat no more. The father stood before her, eyes glazed with booze or pills. The father looked down at the sink, seeing the locket there. He reached past her and picked it up. 'Fuck is this?' the boy saw him say. 'Huh?' Then he slapped her. Blood boiled in the boy. He saw red, a red deep and bloody and filled with fury. Murderous red. It came back to him for the second or third time in his life, the capacity to do murder. He jumped down from the ledge and over the balcony, and leapt onto the downspout and tore up the two stories to his balcony. He rushed inside. Falling to the floor he reached an arm under his bed, pulling out a trunk and throwing it open. Buried at the bottom of the trunk was the kukri. He took it out and tested the weight of it in his hand.

When the front door of his apartment was kicked in, he jumped. Then the sound of his mother screaming. Aurora's father, come to take it out on him. Let him. The boy was ready. The boy would kill the fucker and free the girl. He raised the knife, opened the door and went outside. But it was not the girl's father he saw, but two men he didn't know. There was no doubting the intention in their eyes. On the floor in front of them was his mother. He looked from the men to her, and back at the men. Then he turned and ran back into the room, snapping the lock shut and fleeing onto the balcony. Thoughts of the girl were pushed to the back of his mind. Fight or flight. He was not the only one with murder in his heart; he'd seen it in the eyes of his mother's attackers. He leapt to the balcony across the alley from his, a jump he'd never made before, but now, faced with life or death, he made it without thinking. Once across, he used the AC unit to leap to the balcony above, and the same to reach the ledge of the roof.

The first shot came as he was pulling himself over the ledge. He heard the crack and felt the impact on the wall, and the whinny of the bullet as it ricocheted off the mortar. He fell, rolled, and sprinted across the roof. At the far end he made the jump without pause, rolling when he hit the ground. Running again. Furiously. The body the decisionmaker. Adrenalin. Drive. Then the second shot. Right as he reached the ledge. And instead of rising up and over, he tumbled, his body careening over the edge. Bullet through the heart.

The shooter made the leap over the gap between the buildings closely followed by his accomplice. They crossed the roof and peered over. Below lay the boy, on his face on an iron walkway a story down.

'Go and look,' the shooter said.

The man walked to the end of the building where a staircase gave onto the walkway below. He descended and approached the boy and opened the backpack, taking out the operabox and holding it up for his partner to see.

'Got it.'

The other nodded. 'Let's go.'

Saleh heard it.

Having traveled with the boy most of the way home, the sound of the shot that killed his friend reached his ears. He followed the sound and passed like a ghost in the dark of night, an apparition of the city's dreamtime. He first found the spent cartridge then blood, then discovered the body of his friend, the backpack lying open. He touched Caleb's cold face. Sat down and put his head in his hands. Cursed. Then he got up and lifted the body of his friend.

When he got to the flat the door was hanging on its hinges. He went inside carrying Caleb and found his mother in the kitchen bleeding from the head, and when she saw her boy she howled a terrible animal cry which made Saleh weep. He placed his friend on the kitchen table and Caleb's mother sat down, gripped her son's arm and did not let go. She put her head on the boy's shoulder and wept. Saleh, spent and in shock, went into his friend's room and lay down. In moments he was asleep.

8

When he woke, Saleh did something that for the rest of his life he would never be able to explain. He sat up and put his feet on the floor. His eyes alighted on the pipe on the shelf. He got up, crossed the room and picked up the pipe. Then he unscrewed it. The SD card fell to the floor. He picked it up and looked at it, then slipped it into his pocket.

The boy's mother was still sitting at the kitchen table with her dead son. Her face wracked with grief, she did not register Saleh's presence. The boy put an awkward hand on her shoulder and she looked up at him in surprise. It took a moment for her eyes to focus.

'I think we should call the police,' he said. She didn't reply. 'Do you need more time?'

She shook her head.

The police came. Took statements. Searched the house, took fingerprints. Sent her dead son in an ambulance to the morgue, then brought the two of them to the police station where they were interrogated. After they took Saleh to the roof where the boy was shot, took photos and searched the place, and when they were done it was almost six in the morning.

The flat was sealed up and the boy's mother put in a hotel. The very next morning, she was at the morgue to see her son, and stayed there until she was told to leave. She returned to the cell-like confines of her hotel room.

Saleh disappeared. Took to the roofs and vanished. Lost in her grief, the woman didn't give much thought to the boy who'd carrried her dead son's body to her. But as the weeks passed and she moved back to the apartment, she wondered about him. Her son's absence was more than she could bear. In the beginning she slept in his bed so that she might fall asleep with his scent on her. No perfume it was, but for all that a lingering reminder of the boy she'd birthed and nurtured and raised, and watched grow into a young man. A life. Gone now into the eternal catacombs of memory and forgetting. For some, grief does not pass. It merely burrows deeper, becomes entrenched; less acute but no less painful. A pain that becomes profound in its abyssal reach.

Months went by like this, and when the woman could bear it no more, she packed up and moved to another apartment in the same block. No progress had been made in her son's case. Daily she made her trips to the police station and to other offices, places where the victims of injustice gathered searching reprieve from their suffering, lawyer's offices and victim support, community groups where scant effort was made to find witnesses to crimes. All came to naught. One after another she lost both the jobs she worked, until she was subsisting on welfare and with the help of her neighbors. Grim determination kept her going. Kept her search alive. Drove her on. No mother who has buried a son ever forgets. Her life, a struggle and with much hardship, had never had such purpose. She was resolute. Her son's killers would face justice, at her own hand if need be.

Then one day, the boy knocked on her door. The woman opened it and saw him there looking sheepish and regretful. For a moment, he was unsure she recognized him. Then she reached out and took him by the hand.

'Hi.'

He smiled apologetically. 'Hi.'

'You'd better come in.' He followed her inside and they went to the kitchen. She put a pot of water to boil and pulled out a chair for him. He sat down. She looked at him, the eyes softening at this boy who occupied a place at her table, filling the hole that had grown from the death of her child.

'I don't even know your name,' she said.

'Saleh.'

'Saleh.' She nodded, and said it again. 'Were you a friend of Caleb's?'

Saleh nodded.

'You know, it's like I didn't even know him. I'd never even met you before. He even kept Aurora a secret from me.'

'Aurora?'

'Yeah – this girl he liked, downstairs. Sweet girl.' She turned, taking two mugs from the sink and spooning coffee into them.

'Philippines,' the boy said.

She turned. 'What?'

'The Philippines. He wanted to take her to the Philippines.'

She looked at him, brow furrowed. 'He said that?'

The boy nodded.

She dropped the spoon on the counter, covered her eyes with her face and began to weep profusely. Her shoulders heaved with the violence of her grief. The boy squirmed nervously on the chair. He did not know where to look. Eventually, forced by mere awkwardness to rise, he got up and went over and put his arms around her weakly. She clung to him and sobbed into his shoulder.

'God, I'm sorry,' she blubbered. 'So sorry…'

The boy cleared his throat nervously. She let off her desperate embrace and wiped her eyes, then turned to the mugs and filled them with hot water. She took the cups and set them on the table. She sat down.

'It's like I hardly knew my own son.'

Saleh sat. She wiped her eyes with the balls of her palms and took out a tissue.

'I didn't know him so well either,' Saleh said. 'He was very... closed.'

She nodded. 'He had a difficult early life. You know, with his dad and whatever. He buried lots of things. Kept them hidden from me. It was his way of protecting himself from pain.'

The boy sipped the coffee, put the mug down and stared at the table.

'I never thanked you, for what you did that night. Bringing him back to me. Thank you.' She began to weep again but quickly forced herself to stop. 'You know, it was important that time I had with him before they took him away. It wouldn't have been the same if I'd been called down to the morgue to find him there, dead.' She forced a smile, her eyes wet. 'It meant a lot to me.'

The boy nodded. 'They still don't know what happened?'

She shook her head. 'The police told me they were looking for you, but they couldn't find you.'

'I'm sorry. There are some things, family things. I couldn't have the police coming to where I live. Too many problems.'

She nodded. 'That's okay. There was nothing else you could tell them anyway.'

He hesitated, taking a sip of coffee and putting his mug down. 'There might be one thing...' He put his hand in his pocket and took out the SD card and pushed it across the table. 'I don't know, I don't even know for sure what's on it, but it might be something.'

She picked it up. 'What is it?'

'It's a program for a device called an operabox. Very expensive, very high-tech. Caleb stole it, I think, and this might have been in it when he stole it. Or, it might be something else. I don't know.'

She furrowed her brow. 'And you think this might have something to do with why he was killed?'

He shrugged. 'I'm not sure. It might be something. But you'll need to find someone who knows about these things.'

'Like who?'

'I can take you to this guy I know. He might be able to help.'

'A scientist?'

Saleh shook his head. 'A computer guy. You gotta know that this thing might be illegal, and this guy kinda works off-grid. Backstreets kind of thing.' He pointed at the card. 'I don't know what's on there, but it's not something you wanna look into yourself.'

She looked at him then put the SD card down on the table. She was quiet for a long time as she stared at it.

'Do you want to meet him?' Saleh said.

She looked at him, fire in her eyes once more. 'Yes. Yes I do.'

9

'This is the most fucked-up thing I've ever seen.' The man put the card on the counter and folded his arms. He looked wearied, like he'd been down the long dark night of the soul and only just come out the other side. 'I never wanna see that shit again. That took twenty fucking years off my life.'

Celeste looked at him, the fire in her eyes that of one who'd been given a glint of hope, a crumb in the search for her son's murderers. Beside her, Saleh sat quietly.

'What is it?' she said.

'My best guess, it's a program that simulates hell. I mean, real fire and brimstone, demon-with-a-burning-stick-up-your-ass hell.' He shook his head. 'No one, and I mean *no one*, needs to see that.'

Celeste sat back and stared at the man. Saleh had taken her to this back-alley computer chopshop in the seediest corner of the Mercantile district. This was not the kind of man she'd ever dealt with before, but in the circumstances, she had no qualms about being there. He chewed on his mustache nervously, eyes blinking as if stinging with salt.

'Who would make such a thing?'

The man took a deep breath, sat forward and clasped his hands together. 'When I plugged this card into my system and turned it on, my firewalls went fucking bananas. This thing is high-tech, as advanced as it gets. Luckily, I got protection, or there might be a man at my door right now. I might be fucking dead.'

Celeste began to put the picture together. 'A company made this...'

He nodded. 'I was able to retrieve a signature from the source code, and believe me, it was buried deep. Whoever created this did not intend it to go public. It's a beta release, not fully developed—'

'Who?' said Celeste.

'A company called Vathos.'

'Never heard of them.'

'You wouldn't have. They fly very low under the radar, nobody knows a great deal about them.'

'Do you? Know something, I mean?'

He shook his head. 'Only rumors. Look, if you're going to pursue this, I have to warn you, these are the kind of people that do not take kindly to scrutiny. Nobody knows for sure what they do. And to be honest, I don't wanna fucking know what they really do...'

'You gotta give me something. Please...'

The man bowed his head. When he raised it, Saleh saw he was afraid for the woman.

'Look, I might know someone who can help you, but these are dangerous people. They have good intentions, sure, but they're on watchlists. Some of them are in hiding. If you get into bed with these people, you're never gonna be able to get on a plane again. You may have to change your name, your identity. I'm just sayin—'

'I wanna find who killed my son.' The look in her eyes was adamantine.

He gestured to Saleh. 'The boy told me what happened. I feel for you. I'm just trying to warn you what's gonna happen should you go down this road. That's all I can do.'

'I was already decided, before I even walked in the door. I'll die if it means justice for my son.'

The man took a deep breath. He lifted a piece of paper and a pencil from inside a desk organizer and scratched out a phone number, then wrapped the SD card in it and pushed it across the counter.

'From here on in, I'm out. I have to insist you never come back here with that thing. And if anyone asks, and they well might, you never came here and you never met me.'

Celeste nodded. She opened the bag she was holding and took out a purse. 'How much do we owe you?'

The man held up his hands. 'I don't want your money. Honestly, I hope you find what you're looking for. But for fuck's sake, think twice before you go down this road.'

Celeste and Saleh sat across from one another at the kitchen table in the apartment. The piece of paper lay unfolded on the table and next to it, her phone. Saleh sat waiting.

'Do you think he was telling the truth?' she said.

'About the company? And maybe getting into trouble?'

She nodded.

'I guess. I mean, I dunno, but he really seemed like he was scared.'

'I'm not afraid for myself, I'm not. I'm scared for you. If I'm gonna do this, I think you need to leave and not come back here.' Her eyes were filled with a sadness that overwhelmed the boy. 'Honestly, if you walk out now and don't turn around, I won't feel the least bit angry at you. I've already lost a son. I don't need the death of another boy on my hands.'

Saleh looked at her without saying anything. He turned to look at the door but didn't rise, and when he turned back to Celeste he merely shrugged. 'He was my only friend. I want to help you find the people who did this.'

She smiled and nodded, and reached across the table to take his hand in hers. 'Thank you. I mean that. With all my heart.'

The boy blushed. Then she picked up the phone and dialed the number.

It rang exactly twice and was answered. The voice gave only a curt 'Yes?'.

'Hello.' The woman was suddenly without words.

'Yes?'

'Someone gave me your number.'

'I think you have the wrong number, lady. Goodb—'

'Wait!'

On the other end of the line, silence.

She blurted out, 'I think Vathos killed my son.'

Quiet followed. And then, 'I'm not sure I know who you think you're talking to.'

She rubbed her temples. 'I... I want to help you.' And then, 'I want you to help me.' She heard a sigh.

'Right. Who are you?'

Celeste was unfamiliar with the Village, just across the bridge from Chinatown. A taxi took them to Stanton Road, and from there it was on foot. It was Wednesday, about seven, and Celeste followed Saleh into the pedestrianized streets. Quaint, bohemian, it was a far cry from her encounter in the backstreet chopshop. Shops were just closing and dusk was upon them. The setting gave her small confidence that they were not walking to their deaths at the hands of some corporate security team.

They made their way to Christie Square, where they'd been instructed to sit down and have a coffee and set a red carrier bag on the table to mark themselves. They did so. Celeste bought two coffees and they sat down, neither of them touching the cups.

'Are you afraid?' the boy said.

Celeste looked at him and sighed. 'As long as we're in public, I think we're okay. Right?' The boy's face tensed at her reply. She put a hand on his arm. 'We'll be fine. Don't worry.'

They sat for almost twenty minutes, now and again looking about them to see if they were being watched, which they almost certainly were.

'Try not to look so nervous,' Celeste said.

Celeste picked up the coffee and took a sip. It was lukewarm. No sooner had she put it down than a man passed their table, pausing only long enough to say under his breath: 'Leave the coffee and follow me.'

He didn't even make eye contact. Celeste, heart hammering, stood up and the boy did so too. They followed the man in the charcoal army coat across the square and into an adjoining alley.

'What happens if we're no longer in public?' Saleh whispered as they hurried after the man.

'Then we pray these are good people.'

The boy looked up at her, saw the resolve on her face. She wouldn't go back. Probably there was no going back.

At the end of the alley the man turned left, and after a hundred meters turned right into a shabby arcade. The arcade was filled with makeshift streetfood stalls, hawkers of cheap jewelry and drug paraphernalia stands. They followed him through to the other side, coming out onto a car park which they crossed, cutting through a fence and onto an embankment. The man ran up it and they followed, and found themselves on the off-ramp of the bridge. A car was waiting. The man opened the back door and beckoned them to enter. Celeste ducked to try to get a look at the driver.

'Now's not the time for second thoughts,' the man holding the door said.

She looked at him. He was wearing sunglasses and there was no way to read his intent. She was entirely at the mercy of faith. She turned once to look at the boy, who nodded, then they both clambered into the car. The man shut the door and jumped in the front seat. The car took off across the bridge as the woman sat clutching the red carrier bag that contained only scrap paper, as if it contained the secret of life.

The car pulled into an alley, best Celeste could guess somewhere in the Mercantile district. They'd traced a serpentine weave across the city, the female driver and her accomplice vigilant every step of the way. They'd even stopped under a bridge to search the woman and the boy, and scan them too, and only when they'd established they were free of any tracking devices had they continued. Now they got out of the car in the dark dead-end of an alley, looming above which was a five-story building that at one time may have been a mill or a factory. No sooner had they stepped out of the car than a steel door opened and a man appeared there. He was dressed shabbily. He held the door open, gesturing inside. The woman and the boy entered.

The door slammed shut. They all regarded each other warily, the woman and the boy with the man in front of them, behind them the pair who'd ferried them from the Village.

'You're Celeste,' the man said.

She nodded.

'I read about your son. A tragedy. I'm very sorry. You realize we had to do a little research into you before we agreed to meet.'

'Yes.'

He turned to the boy. 'And you're Saleh.'

The boy cleared his throat but didn't say anything.

'We couldn't find out so much about you. You're a bit of a ghost, kid.'

'I lost my parents. I live with relatives.'

'Do you now?' The man eyed him intently.

The woman sidled closer to Saleh. 'He's just a boy.'

The man nodded. 'Doesn't matter though, does it? If we don't scrutinize everyone we encounter, we risk our lives.' He turned to the boy. 'Luckily we have a contact at juvenile detention and we know you've been lifted for trespassing a number of times. Trespassing is a crime we can get behind.' The man almost smiled. 'Trespassing is something we hold in high regard.'

Saleh held the man's gaze. 'I never stole anything. Never.'

'Good.' This time, the man really did smile. 'Honest too.'

He turned to Celeste. 'Look, we know why you're here. But do *you* know why you're here?'

'I want to find my boy's killers.'

'Yes, I know. But do you know what we do?'

She shook her head. The man glanced over her shoulder at the man and woman behind her. 'Take them through. We'll sit down and talk.' He looked at Celeste. 'Just know that we aren't committed to helping you in any way. Yet.'

Celeste looked defiant, but a flash of fear crossed her eyes. She nodded.

'Alright.' The man turned. 'Follow Eva.'

They took her to a room somewhere deep in the building. The room was semi-derelict like much of the rest of the place: crumbling plaster on the walls, floor half-rotted through in the corners, windows smashed and boarded up in places. Celeste saw through a door at the rear of the room, which looked onto an enormous machine of some description, a printing press was her best guess. The woman who'd driven them there gestured to a chair and Celeste sat down, Saleh next to her. The two men entered the room, their escort standing by the door with his arms crossed. The man they'd found there sat down in front of them.

'What we're going to tell you is some of what we know about Vathos operations in this country and around the world. What is undeniable is that they kill to protect their business. Anyone who gets close ends up dead. All of us here – Marko, Eva, and me – we've lost people to the company. Eva lost her husband, Marko a brother. I lost my son.'

'Why has nobody stopped them?'

'At the level they're operating at, there has to be state complicity in what they're doing. There's no other way for them to survive. They're protected, and at a very high level.'

The woman began to ask another question, but the man held up a hand.

'Just listen, and I'll explain what I know best I can, then

you can ask any questions you have. Okay?' She nodded. 'So, we've put together all we know based on research, personal experience, and a whole lot of conjecture. Only recently we've experimented with hacking their systems, but they've got some of the tightest security we've ever seen. Vathos are a company with very deep pockets and a very extensive reach. So far as we know they operate in all of the G7 countries, possibly the G20 too. They specialize in and facilitate espionage, and not only that, they seem to be involved in subversion, definitely politically and possibly corporate too. They interfere in political processes and elections, steer public policy, create the conditions for favorable economic outputs, even facilitate conditions for kinetic warfare if it's in someone's interest. And how do they do all this? By hacking the minds of people in power so that they can manipulate them and have them do their bidding. We don't know the details of how they do it, but we know they use very advanced AI to penetrate people's minds and create conditions that make them easy to manipulate. Like I say, we only have piecemeal information, but what we know is terrifying.'

'And nobody knows about this?' Celeste still clutched the red carrier bag.

He shook his head. 'No. And why? Because they cover their tracks by killing anyone who might be able to testify about what they do.' He turned to the woman, who leaned against a battered desk. 'Eva's husband was a mid-level engineer at a computer security firm. One day he was running some routine security at Escalate VR when he chanced upon a pretty fucked-up program buried in the company's archives. He reported it to his superiors, and not long after that he became aware of being followed. Two weeks later he was dead. A "mugging" is what they dressed it up as, but we know the truth. There was no mugging. It was a hit.' He paused. 'What is it they're saying about your son's killing?'

Celeste shook her head. 'They're saying he broke into someone's house and was shot by the owner.'

He nodded. 'And you will never get the full story from the police, I'm sorry to tell you. But we are fighting to bring out the truth.'

'And who are you exactly?' Celeste said.

'Like I say, that's Marko and Eva, my name is Eric. We operate as a loose conglomerate of people who are committed to bringing out the truth about Vathos and their operations.'

'Is it just you?'

He shook his head. 'There are others. But it's better I don't say more about that now.'

Celeste nodded. She turned to Saleh, who seemed a little lost. She tried to reassure the boy with her eyes.

Eric leaned forward. 'The man who gave you the phone number, he said something about a card. Did you bring it with you?'

Celeste put her hand in her pocket and took out the card still wrapped in the piece of paper. She handed it to him. Eric slipped a hand in the inside pocket of his jacket and took out a pair of glasses. He put them on and unwrapped the paper and examined the card.

'We'd like to have a closer look at this. You mind if we keep it for a little bit? If this truly is from Vathos, it could give us insights into what they do that we can only dream of.'

Celeste nodded. 'Take it. Keep it. I wouldn't even know what to do with it. The man who looked at it said it was the worst thing he ever saw.'

'He told me. We're very curious to see it. A little afraid too. But we need to examine it – it could be a massive help to us.'

He turned and held it out, and Marko approached and took it from his hand, slipping it into the breast pocket of his army coat. Eric turned back to Celeste and Saleh.

'Knowing what you've heard, about us, about what we've gone through, that we've lost people and may lose our own lives, and that if you want to help us, you too might end up dead – do you still want to know more? Because you can walk out that door now and you'll never see or hear from us again.'

Celeste and Saleh turned to look at each other. They'd only recently drifted into each other's orbit and barely knew each other, but the look they shared communicated a common cause and understanding, that they were now into something they did not fully comprehend and was indeed a threat, perhaps fatal, but above all they were in it together. They were bound by the death of one who was dear to both of them.

They turned and gave their silent assent to this stranger.

'Good. And you understand that us helping you means you helping us?'

'Yes.'

'Alright. In that case, there's some things you're gonna have to get familiar with. Things that will get unpleasant very quickly, for the both of you.' He stood up. 'This is going to get dirty.'

*

'I'm not sure about this,' Celeste said, putting a hand on Eva's arm.

They'd travelled in back of a van to an unknown location, Celeste and Saleh together. Now they were somewhere in the city, in a cramped basement filled with computers and hardware, and she was in a seat with Eva getting ready to plug something into her neck. If she wasn't afraid, she was certainly freaked out. She looked over at Saleh, who sat in the seat next to her.

'It's okay to be scared,' he said.

'Who's he, and what's he doing?' Celeste pointed at the man in front of the consoles.

Eva put her hand on Celeste's. 'We told you. That's Verne. He's the operator.'

'Operating what?'

Eric entered the basement, closing the door behind him. Eva turned to see him enter, throwing him a look of concern. He took off his coat and draped it over a chair, pulling the chair over to where Celeste and Saleh sat waiting to be plugged into the system. He clasped his hands together and looked at her intently.

'Remember what we talked about?' he said.

'Yes.' She nodded. 'But I wasn't ready for all this. I have no idea what this stuff does, what it'll do to me... you're about to plug something into me. All my life I never had use for anything other than my phone. Now I see all these computers, all these screens, and I've no idea what's about to happen.'

The man turned to Saleh. 'You've used VR before, right?' Saleh nodded. 'Well, it's a bit like VR, except more real. Was the VR scary?'

'A little bit.'

'So, what you're about to do now is a bit scary, but only because it's unfamiliar to you.' He turned back to Celeste. 'You agreed you would be able to help us in operations, and we've got this one operation we think you might be perfect for, but before we go down that road we need to familiarize you with the metaconsciousness, what we call "System A", or "SISTEMA". That's what we're doing here today. We're not gonna drop you in anywhere scary, we're just gonna set you free to go and do some exploring. And you'll be together, so you won't be out there on your own and confused and lost and afraid.'

'Are you sure it's safe?'

'One hundred per cent.'

Celeste looked at Saleh. 'Are you ready to do this?'

He nodded. She held out her hand and he took it and squeezed.

'When all is said and done, it's really quite beautiful down there. Or *up* there. We can't really fathom the full extent of it, or how it ultimately relates to our consciousness as human beings. It's wondrous. But Vathos are using it for dark purposes, and that's why we need to fight them using their own methods. SISTEMA is a place of dreams, but the origin of all nightmares too.'

'Please don't give me any nightmares,' Celeste said.

Eric smiled. 'Not today.' He looked from Celeste to Saleh. 'So, are you ready?'

She took a deep breath and nodded. 'Okay. Let's do this.'

Eva leaned in to apply the epidural.

Eric stood up. 'Good. Get ready to enter System A.'

CONTINUE WITH PART THREE...

THE SISTEMA SERIES

1. CEREBRUM

Subconscious torture for political and corporate subversion. That's the trade of Vathos—creeping into a target's dreams to force the shady ends of their clients. It's dirty business.

Vangelis Zervas is one of their Subversion agents and makes a living inflicting pain on people in their sleep. A recipient of the most stringent training and a man of few qualms, he'll do whatever it takes to get the job done. But when a series of events calls his dedication into question, strange things begin to happen when he infiltrates the dreams of his targets. Soon he's asking himself—is it he in the mark's head, or is someone else in his?

A no-holds-barred dystopian horror that will put your teeth on edge.

2. ACOLYTE

Caleb, a young school dropout, robs an apartment one night with his petty-criminal friend, Vince. Finding an expensive and rare piece of computer hardware, he pockets it, oblivious to its power and purpose. The boy plugs himself into the new device, unaware that the program inside it is a diabolical piece of software, one which almost kills him. But those who created the program do not want it out in the world and will do anything to retrieve it, including killing anyone in whose possession it is found. Caleb may find that by taking the device he has unwittingly unleashed forces that will consume all he knows and loves.

3. CHIMERA

Following the murder of her young son, Celeste goes all in with a group of co-conspirators to infiltrate Vathos, the company she believes responsible for the death of her child. The faction make tentative contact with Vangelis Zervas, hoping he will help them penetrate the Vathos servers so they may gather evidence to bring the company down. Despite the nature of his ruthless and horrific work, Vangelis may have his own misgivings with the company. But is it enough for him to turn on Vathos?

In the end, he may have only one choice: Hell or death.

4. INFERNO

After a penetration operation on the Vathos servers goes awry, Celeste and Vangelis Zervas are cast into the Vathos mainframe following a possible sabotage operation from within the company. The pair are drawn into the 'Inferno' program, a devious piece of software long held in the companies archives, the program a digitalized recreation of Hell itself. Celeste and Zervas are pursued by Maynes, who, having discovered that the agent has gone rogue, is hell-bent on retribution. But no one gets through Inferno unscathed. Evil begets evil, and soon Celeste and Zervas will come face to face with something far darker, and far more sinister than Maynes.

5. DIABLO

Within every man is a devil. There is only one Satan.

Vangelis Zervas has just been subjected to the most insidious psychological program ever invented by man. He comes out of it in a coma, sequestered in the Medical wing at Vathos systems. Maddox Maynes, his supervising officer, has also returned from their encounter in 'Inferno', still conscious but carrying something deeply sinister within him. The reverberations of the program are carried from the virtual into the real, as Vathos is shaken from within by the greatest enemy it will ever face. This is the beginning of the end.

OTHER HORROR BY ULTAN BANAN

LITTLE SWINE

A small basement cell. A dirty bed. A chair.

These are the confines of Little Swine's world. Prisoner of Momma and subject to the tortures of Boy, her life is a living hell.

Momma has a plan. Momma wants a baby that she may redeem the sins of her past. This is Little Swine's purpose. And when Momma has what she wants, Little Swine will be discarded.

But violence begets violence and blood begets blood, and many will die before the devil has his quota. One can never underestimate the power of retribution.

THE COTTAGE

Men are men until they encounter evil. And after, they are compelled to do evil itself.

Turning their backs on New York, John and Katie Mears purchase their dream home in colonial Connecticut, the place they hope to raise their firstborn and build life as a family. But the cradle of the American nation has a haunting past, and they find themselves swallowed by a dark history, one of blood and anguish, a specter of the country's painful birth in the slaughter of pilgrim times. The dark crucible of the nation is yet manifest. Blood debt is eternal, and sooner or later history calls for retribution. It is the blood of innocents that pays for the sins of the father.

MEAT

In the murky wake of the financial crisis a string of establishments pop up across Europe catering to a hedonistic underground, its clientele beholden to a strange, hallucinatory meat. Stoked by the fleshy and charismatic Hugo and fuelled by voracious consumption of ecstasy, the craze spreads from the heart of Europe all the way to the Mediterranean, where in Athens the financial elite begin to turn on each other. Murder, barbecue and apocalyptic raving ensues, culminating in the most savage party Mykonos has ever seen. Follow the story to its destructive end, where consumption eats itself alive.

NOTES FROM A CANNIBALIST

1847. Assuming the identity of a dead Jesuit priest, a survivor of the famine in Ireland travels to South America where he is tasked with rebuilding the missions among the natives. Inducted into local life, Father James Carmichael finds love with a native woman and becomes acquainted with the ways of the Guaraní, discovering ayahuasca and ritualism. In a battle with his own gods and demons, the priest fights for the life he envisions, his own self the ultimate stake of the struggle. Worlds are shattered, realities crumbled, lives destroyed. His soul victim to the crucible of the New World, what is tempered in the chaos will be outside his control.

A WHORE'S SONG

Hidden away in the backstreets of Amsterdam is a secretive whorehouse, open only to those in the know, where torture, pain and extreme sexual sport are the vehicle to understanding and self-knowledge. Run by the obscure Madame Zhu, the establishment is a magnet to the city's elite and mad soul-seekers alike. Two lives collide in a chaotic downward spiral brought about by psychoactives and sexual torture when, over the course of a day, a whore recounts her life as a destroyer of egos and one man is forced to face his deepest demons. Cast out into the far reaches of his mind, will he make it back from the other side?

In a world where the weak become prey and strength means brutality, living may come at the cost of dying first.

The Book of God

God has lost the plot. He spends his days in the trees killing birds, or crawling through the bushes to watch humans at their rut. His only companion and sole remaining attendant, a withered and tortured scribe, chronicles the Lord's descent into madness as he struggles to bring order to *The Book of Souls*, a record of every being that has ever passed and the reason for the Lord's suffering. But when the Scribe is forced to hire a maid to aid in the care of the Almighty, the introduction of a buxom woman into God's life brings chaos in its wake. Suffering rejection, humiliation and loathing of humankind, God seeks a way to bring back Christ and trigger the Apocalypse.

The Book of God is a work of prose, poetry and black humour that casts an irreverent eye on the holy trinity of sex, death and madness.

The Jaguar

1849. Salome Azul, daughter of a powerful politician, flees Buenos Aires at the height of the Argentinian civil war. In London she enlists the help of Irishman Sean Ryan to open The Nightingale, a high-class brothel and opium den that will be used to entrap and blackmail London's political elite.

In doing so she will make enemies. What's more, Ms. Azul has carried her own demons from Argentina, and it is these that will prove her most relentless foe. In order to survive, she must eliminate all weakness from her character. Doing so may mean cutting away all she cherishes most.

In the pursuit of power, unrelenting sacrifice is what decides who lives and dies.

WORKS OF TRANSLATION BY ULTAN BANAN

Pietro Aretino's Dialogues

Nanna has been a nun. She's been a wife. She has also been a courtesan. And now, as her daughter turns sixteen, she must decide how to advise on her path in life. On what route should she send young Pippa?

Bawdy, filthy, hilarious and uproarious, listen to Nanna regale her friend Antonia with scandalous tales—tales of seduction, blasphemy, lies, dishonesty, thievery, nastiness, cruelty and treachery—in an attempt to decide on what course to set her daughter: should she be a nun, a wife or a whore?

Ultan Banan started writing as a way of getting his head straight, discovering in the process that staying busy is the only way to stop oneself going insane. He devotes what time he can to writing, doing his best to avoid gainful employment by increasingly creative means. He lives on the move but dreams of a small cottage on a foul and inhospitable coast somewhere. Currently in Scotland.

Latest news at
ultanbanan.com

Substack:
ultanbanan.substack.com

Twitter:
twitter.com/ultanbanan

www.ingramcontent.com/pod-product-compliance
Lightning Source LLC
Chambersburg PA
CBHW032021180726
48283CB00008B/2780